M000195482

CODE NAME:

RANGER

K19 SHADOW OPERATIONS

BOOK ONE

USA TODAY BESTSELLING AUTHOR

HEATHER SLADE

CODE NAME: RANGER
© 2021 Heather Slade

All rights reserved. No part of this book may be used or reproduced in any manner whatsoever without written permission, except in the case of brief quotations embodied in critical articles and reviews.

This book is a work of fiction. The names, characters, places and incidents are products of the writer's imagination or have been used fictitiously and are not to be construed as real. Any resemblance to persons, living or dead, actual events, locale or organizations is entirely coincidental.

Paperback: 978-1-953626-56-1

MORE FROM AUTHOR HEATHER SLADE

Table of Contents

Prologue

Ranger

The moment the person briefing us on our next assignment said a serial killer was targeting daughters of wealthy families in the area, I thought of Maisie. She fit the victim's profile better than anyone.

It defied logic, but my gut was telling me to get next door, where I'd left her less than thirty minutes ago, and see with my own eyes that she was safe.

She had to be. My brother was with her. And my teammate Onyx's girlfriend. Or was she his fiancée? Either way, Maisie, Jimmy, and Blanca were fine. Once I confirmed it, I'd come back and we could resume our meeting.

I went to the kitchen and looked out the window. *"No!"* I shouted when I saw the door to the camp swinging open. Why was the fucking door open? It was the middle of winter.

I drew my gun as I raced to have my worst fears confirmed. Both Jimmy and Blanca were gagged, blindfolded, and tied to chairs.

"Where the hell is Maisie?" I shouted at Jimmy as another guy in our unit untied him while Onyx did the same with Blanca.

"They took her," Blanca cried as soon as the gag was out of her mouth.

"Who?"

"Two men. Dressed all in black. Ski masks," Jimmy said between gasps of air. "Used tasers."

"He's been hit." Wasp, the man who'd untied him, pointed to the blood seeping into the fabric of my brother's shirt. I took a step to the side when my boss, Doc Butler, a physician's assistant, rushed over.

"Is there anything else you remember?" I could hear Onyx's words, but they were muffled by the roar of blood surging through my body. Every inch of my skin felt as though it was being pricked by a thousand pins as my brain triggered a fight-or-flight response.

I'd felt it before, more times than I could count, but this was different. This wasn't fear for myself. Someone had taken Maisie, and it was up to me to find her. Save her. Before it was too late.

1

The sun was just coming up when I took a cup of coffee out to the screened-in porch of the lakefront camp—as everyone called the houses and cabins in this part of the world. This place had been in my family for generations and was as good as mine now. My parents rarely came up here once they made Florida their permanent residence. My older brother, Jimmy, had recently separated from his wife and was living here too, but I expected they'd soon reconcile. Since they had kids, I'd thought they would by Christmas for sure, but it hadn't worked out that way.

Looking out at the frozen lake, a chill coursed through my body. It wasn't the frigid temperatures that caused it, though. Instead, it was due to the ever-present feeling of dread that had settled in the pit of my stomach three weeks ago when I learned the team of agents and operatives I worked with at K19 Security

Solutions was the target of a mass-murder plot—myself included.

While the firm's founding partners worked to neutralize the threat, the rest of us had been ordered to shelter in the small town until further notice.

It had been years since I went this long without an assignment, and I was antsy. Particularly given I'd recently been tapped as second-in-command of K19's newest unit, Shadow Ops.

A light went on in the camp next door, where Montano "Onyx" Yáñez, the new team's leader, was staying. The place was owned by Blanca Descanso, a woman he was involved with but who had been taken into protective custody elsewhere, given the threat on our lives.

To help pass the time, Onyx and my brother were renovating the place for her, making it fit to live in during the Adirondack's long winters.

Onyx and I weren't the only two people from Shadow Ops living on Canada Lake's shores. Caleb "Diesel" Jacks, Garrison "Cowboy" Cassidy, and Keaton "Buster" Ford were in a rented place two doors down. Wasp and Swan, both pilots, were staying in a camp next door to them.

Wasp, whose given name was Jasper Theron, was former Air Force and had been recruited to work for the CIA around the same time I was. Aubrey "Swan" Lee had been with the UK's Royal Air Force and MI6 before she resigned from Her Majesty's Secret Intelligence Service and came to work for K19.

The seven of us each had a unique area of expertise. After graduating from Syracuse University's Institute for National Security and Counterterrorism, most of my early assignments for the agency were asset extraction.

Diesel, who'd been assigned as my partner for our first mission for the CIA and every one after that, had graduated from Cornell and was a language savant. Last I knew, he spoke twelve fluently.

"What's happening today?" asked Jimmy, flopping down on one of the porch chairs.

"Shouldn't you be asking Onyx that question?"

"Thought I'd try something different this morning."

I chuckled. "Yeah? Well, my day looks pretty much like yesterday, which looked exactly like the day before." The last time I'd done anything remotely interesting was New Year's Eve, when the owner of the defunct amusement park in town had opened the dance hall above the bathhouse for a private party.

I'd had no idea what to expect and went alone, not even bothering to invite Diesel. Consequently, with only one exception, everyone there was at least thirty years older than me.

I'd tried all night to get a minute alone with my sole contemporary, but given it was her family hosting the event, I was unsuccessful.

Maisie Ann Jones was her name, and I hadn't been able to stop thinking about her since that night. I'd first met her when we were teenagers, but didn't remember her being knockout gorgeous like she was now. I had a vague recollection of attending her eighteenth birthday party and a hot and heavy make-out session.

What I'd give to get my mouth on her pouty, bee-stung lips now. I'd weave my fingers into her tousle-curled, platinum-blonde hair, kiss my way down her tight-but-curvy body, and feast on her bigger-than-a-handful tits. The thought of it made my cock strain against the zipper of my jeans.

My fantasy came to an abrupt end when I heard the front door close and watched Jimmy go next door.

I could go over and help, but every time I did, I ended up doing more damage than good. "Construction really isn't your thing, is it, bro?" Onyx had said, smiling and patting me on the back when Jimmy was ready to throttle me. It was hard to muster up enthusiasm for something I sucked at.

However, other than figuring out a way to while away the hours naked and in bed with Maisie, I couldn't muster up enthusiasm for much else.

"You're up early," said Diesel when I pulled out my phone to answer his call.

"Same as I always am."

"Wanna take the sleds for a ride later?"

Same shit, different day. At least driving snowmobiles around the frozen lake got me out of the camp for a few hours. I could probably count on a few beers and a bite to eat somewhere in town too. "Sure."

When I returned several hours later, my brother and Onyx were in the kitchen, staring at a broken music box.

"Al Jones," I heard my brother say.

"What about him?" I asked.

"His family has owned the Jones Carousel Company for three generations. I heard Maisie is taking it over. She'd be the fourth, or fifth, I guess."

Maisie. Shit, what had it been? A couple of hours since I last thought about her?

"Are you saying Al's family built the carousel at Sherman's Amusement Park?" Onyx asked.

Jimmy nodded. "Not only that, Al's grandfather was Sherman Jones. You know, *Sherman.*" My brother pointed at the music box that belonged to Blanca and that Onyx, who broke it, was trying to piece back together. "He made those too. Not very many, though. I think he only released one a year."

"I had no idea," I said under my breath.

"You weren't around as much as I was when we were growing up. Most of the kids who summered here got jobs either at Sherman's or the Canada Lake Store. This one"—Jimmy turned to Onyx and pointed at me—"was always in some high school sport. It was either football, baseball, or track."

"I played basketball too," I muttered.

"Helluva lotta good that did him. So, who's gonna call Al? Me?"

"I can call him." I jumped at the chance Maisie might pick up the phone and I'd be able to add the sound of her voice to my ongoing fantasies. Instead, when her grandmother, Mary, answered, I explained Onyx's situation.

"Come on over and bring Onyx with you. You know you're always welcome. In fact, if you haven't eaten yet, I've got a big pot of chili and jalapeño cornbread on the stove."

"If it's no trouble…Jimmy is here too."

"Owen Messick, you know you have an open invitation. I'll always pick a full table over an empty one."

After I hung up, I filled Onyx and Jimmy in on our dinner invitation. Not that I'd mention it to them, but I was fairly sure I heard another female's voice in the background that I hoped belonged to Maisie.

"I'll change, and then I'll be ready to go," I said, racing up the stairs, but not before I saw my brother's raised eyebrows. Screw him. I'd made the call; I was just as entitled to go along for dinner as he was.

A few minutes later, we stood at the Jones' door and knocked. When it opened, the air left my lungs as I stared into piercing blue eyes.

"Hi, I'm Maisie Ann. I'm Al's granddaughter," she said. "Come on in."

Before I could say a word, Onyx stepped in front of me. "I'm Montano, but most people call me Onyx." He held out his hand, and she shook it.

I stepped up behind him. "Hey, Maisie. I don't know if you remember me—"

"Ranger Messick, how could I ever forget you? There wasn't a girl in Fulton County who didn't have a crush on you."

"It's sure good to see you again," I said when Jimmy and Onyx were greeted by Al.

"You too." Her alabaster skin turned pink, and she cast her gaze downward.

"I have to ask, Maisie Ann. You said there wasn't a girl in Fulton County who didn't have a crush on me. Does that include you?"

She looked up with a smile that could light up any room and winked. "You know it, Ranger."

"That sure was a romantic thing you did for Blanca," I heard Mary say to Onyx. "I told my husband he should take lessons from you."

Maisie put one hand on her hip. "I'm confused. Onyx, you're with Blanca? I thought Jimmy and her used to be an item."

"That's right. Stole her clean away from him." Onyx nudged my brother with his elbow.

"I don't know why I thought you'd married her."

"I am married—actually, separated—but as far as Blanca is concerned, I haven't seen her since I graduated from high school."

"How did you meet her?" Maisie turned to Onyx and asked.

"I knew her sister."

"Oh." The smile left her face. "Um, what was her name again?"

"Sofia."

Her brow furrowed, not unlike most did when Sofia Descanso's name was mentioned. "That's right."

"She got a bad rap, that one," said Al. "But I'll tell you what; she worked her bottom off for me one summer in order to earn enough money to buy her sister one of those carousel music boxes." Al looked at me, then at Onyx. "Ranger here said something happened to it."

When he took it out of the bag and set it on the table, Mary gasped. "Oh, it's worse than I imagined."

"You don't know the half of it," he said, winding it up.

"I see what you mean." Al picked it up to turn the music off. Thank goodness since it hurt my ears.

"Any advice?"

"Well, let me see." Al put on a pair of glasses and held the horse up to the light. "If you mean to fix it, no."

"Do I have any other options?"

Al shook his head. "These have become quite the collector's items. No two were alike. You could try going on one of those auction sites and see if anybody's got one for sale."

"I was afraid you were going to say that."

"Yeah? Already looked?"

Maisie walked over to her grandfather; Mary did the same. Each put their arm through one of his.

"Gramps, please," she begged.

"Al, you know you have to help him," added Mary.

Al shook his head. "Even if I wanted to, I couldn't make another one." He held up his hands. "Arthritis is too bad."

"Maybe Onyx could assist," my brother suggested.

It took Al a couple of minutes to answer, and all the while, I watched Maisie look at her grandfather imploringly.

Finally, Al motioned for Onyx to follow him down the hallway. I couldn't have been happier when Jimmy followed and Mary went into the kitchen, leaving Maisie and me alone.

"Can I get you anything to drink?" she offered.

"I'll take a beer if you've got one."

"When does anyone on the lake not have beer?" She rolled her eyes and pulled two from the refrigerator. "Glass?"

"Bottle's good."

"They may be a while, if you two want to go sit on the porch and chat while I finish up dinner," suggested Mary.

Maisie led the way, and I followed, watching her high and tight ass that was covered by jeans but that I remembered seeing once or twice in a bikini. Man, I wished it was summer and I could get a glimpse of that hotness again.

"So, *Ranger*, the last time I saw you, I must've been fourteen or fifteen."

I took a step closer and looked into her deep blue eyes. "We both know that isn't true, beautiful. We saw plenty of each other after our first meetup. The last time you *talked* to me, you were fourteen."

"I don't recall you striking up a conversation."

I took a sip of my beer. "Correct me if I'm wrong, but I believe we did something more than converse the night of your eighteenth birthday."

"Oh. Were you there that night?" Her eyes darted to the left, and her cheeks flamed a second time.

I leaned in closer still so my mouth was next to her ear. "I'm heartbroken you don't remember."

She took a step back. "Who's lying now?"

I liked that she admitted she had been, in so many words at least. "I can tell you I've never forgotten it. I was quite taken with you."

Her eyes were wide, and she studied my mouth. "So why didn't you ask me out?"

"I think I did, but you were leaving for college the next day."

"You remember that?"

"There's a lot I recall about you."

"I doubt that includes the first time we met."

"You're wrong. It was on the Canada Lake Store docks, and it was the day before I started working there that summer."

"It was the only summer you did."

"I filled in every now and then, but not as much as I would've liked. I came up every weekend I could, though."

"Dinner's ready," I heard Mary call out from the kitchen.

"Wait," said Maisie when I turned to walk in that direction. "What would've happened if I hadn't left the next day?"

"I can't say for certain, but I can tell you why I showed up at your party."

"Why?"

I turned my body and crowded hers into the doorway. "To claim you as mine, sweet Maisie Ann Jones." I waited for her to laugh or get pissed or have some kind of reaction to my Neanderthal proclamation. She didn't have one besides her breathing accelerating and her pupils dilating—which was exactly what I'd been going for.

"So, Ranger, what have you been up to these last few years?" Mary asked partway through our meal.

"Define last few, or we'll be here all night," said Jimmy, smirking at me from the other side of the table.

"You went to college. Is that right?" Mary added, ignoring my brother. "Where?"

"I started out at the Ranger School in Wanakena, but then transferred to 'Cuse."

"What made you change to Syracuse?" Maisie asked.

I laughed. "Honestly, I was bored out of my mind."

"What did you study there?"

There were far too many things I couldn't divulge to Maisie or her grandparents for me to continue with any detail. "Security and Law. What about you? Did I hear you went to Dartmouth?"

"Graduated summa cum laude." Those were the first words Al had spoken since we sat down to eat.

"Impressive," I said, leaning close enough that my arm touched hers.

"I was always kind of a geek."

"What did you study?" I asked even though I knew the answer, just like I knew she'd graduated with honors.

"Economics, then went on to get my MBA from Tuck."

It was ranked the fifth-best MBA program in the country and the tenth-best in the world.

"And she came back to save the carousel business," said Al, beaming.

"A little more than that," she mumbled, only loud enough for me to hear.

I couldn't wait to ask her what the more was. Given her education, the sky was the limit for Miss Jones. I wouldn't ask now, though. I wanted Maisie to get lost in her response, tell me all her hopes and dreams, while I simultaneously seduced her into my bed. Instead, I changed the subject.

"So, what's the plan for the music box?" I asked, dropping my arm under the table. When Maisie did the same, I took her hand in mine and squeezed. I leaned close and whispered in her ear. "Tomorrow night, just you and me. Sound good?"

She squeezed back and nodded.

"Pick you up at seven."

2

Maisie

As if I had any prayer of sleeping tonight. Nope, that wouldn't be happening. It was as though I'd gone back in time to when I was a teenager, crazy about Owen "Ranger" Messick and absolutely certain he had no idea I was alive.

Did he really remember coming to my birthday party? God, I swear my panties almost melted off my body whenever I thought about kissing him that night and how I wished I hadn't had to leave the next morning. I'd never been kissed like that before or since.

There was just something about being taken back to that time of my life, when the world held endless possibilities, when falling in love at the lake was every teenage girl's dream and nothing mattered beyond who you ended up sitting next to at the bonfire, especially if they gave you a ride home in their boat.

I couldn't help but wonder what might have happened between us if I hadn't gone away to college.

Would he really have asked me out? Would Ranger have taken my virginity instead of the asshole fraternity guy whose name I wished I could forget?

Would I have fallen madly in love and followed him to Syracuse instead of pursuing my own dreams?

God, I hoped not. I'd seen too many of my friends choose to get married instead of going to college, as if the two things were mutually exclusive. Then, two or three kids later, they'd realize they resented missing out on all the things most people experienced in their early twenties. Invariably, those who married right out of high school were divorced by the time they were twenty-five. Of course there were exceptions, but they were statistically rare.

I doubted Ranger was the kind of guy who would've wanted that. Not that I knew much about him. But when he'd mentioned hearing I went to Dartmouth, he sounded impressed. More so after I added that I'd gotten my MBA from Tuck. Then his eyebrows rose, and he smiled.

He'd squeezed my hand in reassurance when my grandfather said I came back to save the carousel business, then whispered he wanted to get together with me tomorrow night—alone.

I couldn't wait.

A little before seven the following evening, my grandmother hollered up the stairwell, "Maisie Ann Jones, stop that pacing or you'll wear a hole in the floor."

"Sorry, Grandma," I hollered back, flopping down on my bed, which didn't exactly make *less* noise. Had I ever been this nervous over a date? Not that I could remember.

Since I had no idea where we were going, I opted for a boho-chic maxi dress that wouldn't make me look like I was trying too hard. I paired it with knee-high boots with a heel, ones I wouldn't normally wear on a date, given the added height made me almost six feet tall. Ranger, though, was at least six four, so I could get away with it.

"Come down and have a glass of sherry before you go," my grandmother said from the bottom of the stairs.

Sherry was her answer to every tense situation. Some said a day out on the lake would take away anything that ailed a person. For her, it was sherry. Summer, fall, winter, or spring—it was always the answer.

A few minutes after I downed my prescribed glass, there was a knock at the door. I wiped my sweaty palms on my dress, but before I could get up to answer it, Grandpa Al pulled it open and invited Ranger inside.

It didn't matter that I'd seen him last night; he still made my heart stop. His dark-brown hair was cut shorter than he used to wear it, but his eyes were still giant pools of warmth I could easily get lost in. His slacks and dress shirt were perfectly tailored, hugging his hard body and making me want to run my hands over every inch.

"Wow," he said, looking me up and down like I was doing to him. "You look gorgeous."

"Thank you." I grabbed my coat from the closet.

"Allow me." He held it so I could ease my arms into the sleeves, then he leaned forward far enough that I could feel his breath on my cheek. "And you smell amazing."

"*Yowza*," Onyx, who I hadn't realized was there, exclaimed with a whistle. "You look beautiful, sis."

I giggled. Was it my imagination, or did I hear Ranger growl?

"Roads are pretty slick out there. Be careful," said my grandfather.

"I sure will. I know exactly how precious my cargo is." Ranger winked. "Ready?"

I kissed the cheeks of both my grandparents, said I loved them, and waved goodbye to Onyx.

"Have fun, kids," he said as we walked out.

"He's such an old soul."

Ranger laughed. "Or a giant five-year-old."

"You two are close."

He nodded. "I would follow him into any battle, anywhere, anytime."

"Powerful words."

"True ones too."

I sensed Ranger was leaving much unsaid, but with the whole night ahead of us, there'd be plenty of time for me to delve deeper.

"Tell me what you're going to save besides the carousel company," Ranger said before we left the driveway.

I laughed. "Wait, I get to ask my questions first."

"Snooze, ya lose, Maisie Ann. Now you'll have to wait your turn."

"Who's the five-year-old? Onyx or you?"

Ranger reached over and squeezed my hand. "I wanna know every single thing there is to know about you, beautiful. Can't fault me for that, can you?"

"I love this place," I said with a smile when he pulled into Dick and Peg's Northwoods Inn several minutes later. Peg, now in her eighties, still did all the cooking and insisted on continuing the tradition of everything being made from scratch.

"Well, if it isn't little Maisie Ann," said Dick, Peg's son, who had been the Northwoods' bartender since he was old enough to see over the counter.

When he came around the bar, I gave him a kiss on the cheek.

"Who's this you've got with you?" he asked.

Ranger stepped forward to shake Dick's hand. "You saw me earlier today, sir. I'm Ranger Messick."

"That's right," Dick nudged him. "You wanted me to save you the fireside table." He waved to the two-top waiting for us. "Come have a drink at the bar first."

That was how it went at the Northwoods Inn. So Peg didn't get too overwhelmed in the kitchen, reservations were mandatory. Every customer was invited to sit at the bar when they arrived. There, they'd look over the menu and place their order. When the first course was ready, Dick would escort them to their table.

I raised a brow when Dick opened a bottle of wine, poured two glasses, and set one in front of each of us. I was more surprised when I asked about the specials and he told me Peg already had our order and our appetizers would be served in a few minutes.

Ranger raised his glass. "To Maisie Ann, savior of the carousel company among other things to be divulged over tonight's dinner."

"To Maisie Ann," said Dick, raising his glass of water.

I touched my glass to theirs and took a sip of one of my favorite wines—that until tonight, I hadn't known Dick carried.

"In case my toast didn't give it away, I'm going to keep pestering you until you tell me."

I took another sip and set my glass on the bar. "I'm surprised you haven't figured it out. It's pretty obvious."

"Humor me."

"Canada Lake, of course."

Ranger smiled and nodded. "Restore the town to its former glory?"

"That's the plan."

"I can't wait to hear all the details."

I cocked my head. "I can't tell if you're serious or joking."

Ranger turned his barstool so he was facing me, leaned forward, and put his arm on the back of my seat. "Completely serious. Tell me how."

I explained that in order to test the theory that I wasn't the only one who longed for things to go back to the way they were when I was growing up, I'd opened the dance hall at Sherman's Amusement Park on New Year's Eve. Tickets sold out in fifteen minutes.

"I know they did. I could only get one."

"You should've called me. I held onto a couple for close friends."

"Would I have rated high enough to score an extra? As a close friend, that is?"

I rolled my eyes. "Of course you would have. Jimmy too."

Ranger put his hand on his heart. "I rank the same as my older brother? *Ouch.*"

"He kept in better touch than you did."

"You got me there. However, I plan to remedy that, here and now." He shimmied his barstool closer to mine.

I looked down to where our legs touched. "That's a good start."

"I like the way you think, Miss Jones." He rested his hand on my knee, and a jolt of desire coursed through my body.

"Yeah?" I leaned forward. Another inch or so, and we'd be close enough to kiss.

"Your table is ready," said Dick, coming up behind us. He reached around and grabbed my wineglass. "Follow me."

I nearly gasped when I saw two steaming bowls of French onion soup waiting for us. "How did you know this was my favorite?"

"I'll never tell," said Ranger, winking. "And neither will Dick."

"Nope, not me. Never seen this guy before in my life."

I shook my head and laughed. Dick and Peg were part of the nostalgia of being at the lake that I longed to bring back. It was one of the few restaurants left in the area. The rest had either closed for the season or for good. For my plan to revitalize the lakeside community to work, having a wide range of places to eat was essential.

"Let's circle back to how you're going to save Canada Lake," Ranger said while we waited for our soup to cool off enough to taste.

"I'd start with the amusement park and the bathhouse, which includes the second-floor dance hall. Once they are fully operational, I'd find investors to renovate the Canada Lake Hotel and make it a destination resort on its own."

"I forgot all about that place. It's just down the shore from Sherman's, right?"

I nodded. "Part of the rehab would be to bring back the boardwalk that connected the two. There used to be shops all along the waterfront—kind of like a miniature Coney Island. There isn't anything like it in the park now, at least not on a shoreline."

"Is that it, or do you have more?"

"Loads more." I broke through the melted cheese on top of the soup and spooned some of the broth, waiting until it stopped steaming before putting it in my mouth. When I did, I groaned. "Food like this, for example.

It's one thing this area needs far more of. Instead of going out to dinner like my parents and grandparents did, my generation meets up at other camps. That's fine and fun, but what about when someone doesn't feel like cooking and cleaning up? Especially when they're on vacation."

"I have to agree. I'm getting pretty tired of the five things my brother and I know how to cook."

I cocked my head. "I'm sure there's more than five."

"Not that we both like. Onyx is a far better cook than either of us are. That's been a bonus."

"Speaking of Onyx…"

3

Ranger

It wasn't that I didn't want to talk about the man. It was more that our professional lives had always been so intertwined that any kind of conversation about him or me would be full of landmines of things I couldn't discuss. "What about the big oaf?" I asked, attempting to begin this conversation on a light note.

"He said he met Blanca through her sister."

"He *knew* her sister."

"Oh. Past tense?"

I nodded. "She passed away."

"My condolences."

"Thanks, but I didn't know her very well."

"She and Blanca were twins, although other than their looks, they never seemed much alike."

"Don't let your favorite soup get cold," I said, motioning with my spoon before taking another bite of mine. I had to admit, I doubted I'd ever had better.

"Is that an attempt to change the subject?"

I rested my spoon on the side of the bowl, picked up my glass of wine, and leaned back in my chair. "Of all the things I know and find fascinating to talk about, Onyx is not one of them."

Maisie set her spoon down like I had and took a sip of her wine. "What about you? Is your life a topic open for discussion?"

My eyes scrunched. "My life? Wow. How about we go back to your plans to save the amusement park instead?"

"I shared my hopes and dreams with you. What are yours?"

"That narrows the subject at least. Let's see. Hopes and dreams." I pushed the tureen of soup back a little and rested my forearms on the edge of the table. "To be honest, I've always dreamed of retiring right here at Canada Lake."

"But?"

I flexed my right hand, then my left. If Diesel were here tonight—instead of Cowboy and Buster, whom he'd assigned to my detail—he'd pick up on my tell. It's what I did when I was stalling.

"I ended up here sooner than I expected to."

"Why?"

I looked into Maisie's eyes and smiled. "Not gonna go easy on me, are you?"

"Would you go easy on me?"

I slowly shook my head and let my eyes drift down her body. "Never."

"I get the feeling we aren't talking about hopes and dreams anymore."

"Sure, we are. Dreams anyway." When I reached across the table, she put her hand in mine. "I dream about kissing you again."

"I dream about it too."

"Yeah? Does that mean you remember I came to your birthday party?"

"I'll never forget it."

I brought her hand to my lips and kissed the back of it.

"Are you finished with your soup? The next course is about to be served," said Dick, feeling the need to refill our wineglasses at the worst moment as far as I was concerned, especially when Maisie took her hand from mine and cleared her throat.

"I'd never let it go to waste," she said, looking up at him.

"Since I am here at Canada Lake, how can I help?" I asked when I took the last spoonful of my hot fudge sundae, evidently the perfect dessert to serve after a stuffed pork chop with green beans, mashed potatoes, and gravy.

"You ordered all my favorites." Maisie leaned back and rubbed her stomach. Unlike me, who polished off every last morsel, she'd saved at least half of everything to take home with her.

"Will you share with your grandparents or keep the leftovers for yourself?"

"With my grandparents? No. With you? Absolutely."

I smiled. "I probably won't be hungry again until tomorrow."

"Works for me." Maisie dipped her spoon into the ice cream and brought it to her mouth. I watched in increasingly excited awe as she lapped it with the tip of her tongue. "You said something about helping?"

"Um…" I flexed both my hands, willing some of the blood in my body to return to my brain so I could think straight enough to respond. "The amusement park. That's where you said you wanted to start, isn't it?"

"Oh, you meant with saving Canada Lake." She dipped her spoon back in the bowl of ice cream.

Maisie Ann Jones was quickly becoming the sexiest woman I'd ever known. "You keep that up, beautiful, and there won't be a single thing in your life I won't help you with."

"Promise?" she asked as I watched her tongue twirl around that damn spoon, unable to think of anything besides her doing exactly that to my cock.

It was at least ten degrees below zero as we walked to the SUV, not to mention I knew we had an audience. They were the only two things stopping me from pushing Maisie up against the outside wall of the Northwoods Inn and thrusting my tongue into her mouth while my hands explored the rest of her body. Once we were inside the vehicle and the heat kicked in, I had no idea how I'd keep my hands off her.

I opened her door, helped her in, and closed it, counting to twenty as I walked around the back of the truck to the driver's side. I climbed in, started the engine, and turned the heaters way up, all without looking at my date, knowing that if I did, I wouldn't be able to stop myself from ravishing her.

"Ranger?" I heard her say above the noise of the fan I'd turned to high.

"Yeah?" I glanced in her direction.

"You aren't going to make me wait until you walk me to my door to kiss me, are you?"

And there went every ounce of my self-control. "Hell, no," I said, reaching for her at the same time she launched herself at me.

Kissing her was every bit as mind-blowingly sexy as I remembered. I gripped the side of her face with my hand, holding her still as my tongue tangled with hers. It was all I could do not to bring both palms to her breasts that were crushed against my chest or slide my hand under her dress and reach up to feel her heat. Instead, I released her.

"Woman, you are killing me."

She rested against her seat. "There are a lot of things I'd like to do to you, Ranger, and not a single one of them ends with you dying."

I had two choices. I could put my hands back on Maisie's body, in which case it might be dawn before we made it out of the parking lot. Or I could put the SUV in gear and take her home.

We were halfway there before I allowed myself to look over at her. As I anticipated, she was looking in my direction. "You have no idea how hard that was, beautiful."

"It's still hard."

Yeah, I could attest to that. The last time I remembered being turned on to the point I ached was eight years ago in this very town with this very woman.

If I stopped at my camp, I'd more than likely toss her over my shoulder, carry her up to my bedroom, and fuck her so hard that neither of us would be able to walk tomorrow. Instead, I ignored her protest when we came to the turnoff and continued straight on the road that led to her grandparents' place.

I pulled in the driveway but left the engine running. Rather than get out, I reached for Maisie, who came into my arms willingly. I kissed her again, just like I had earlier, then rested my forehead against hers.

"Neither one of us is leaving tomorrow, which means we don't need to rush this."

Maisie's eyes bored into mine. "Rush? I feel like I've been waiting my whole life for this."

I couldn't have said it better myself, and that meant we both deserved to savor this moment. Denying each other was difficult, but the intensity building between us would make it worth it.

"I'm going to get out of the truck now and walk you to your door, where I'm going to give you a very chaste kiss good night. If I do anything more than that, I'm afraid Grandpa Al will come out with his shotgun."

"Okay," she whispered, her voice as lust-tinged as I'm sure mine sounded.

When we got close to the back door and I saw Mary watching us from the kitchen, I was grateful I'd worn the winter jacket that was mid-thigh length. Knowing I wasn't strong enough to resist her mouth if our lips touched again, I kissed her forehead.

"Will I see you tomorrow?" she asked as I walked away.

"I'm counting on you bringing those leftovers to my place for lunch. You aren't reneging on that, are you?"

"Only if you want me to come for breakfast instead."

I shook my head and smiled. "Not a minute before noon, Maisie Ann. That's thirteen hours from now. Think you'll be able to make it?"

"Will you?"

When I spun around as if I was going to come after her, she giggled and hurried inside. It was a good thing since Al had joined Mary in the kitchen.

"I wasn't sure we'd see you tonight," said Jimmy, who was sitting in the living room with Cowboy and Buster, all three of them with a beer in hand.

"Yeah, cuz I'm sure Al wouldn't have minded a bit if Maisie invited me in for a sleepover." I glared at the two men who'd knocked off early. "Good thing I made it home okay since I didn't have any backup."

"Sure, you did," said Diesel, walking in the kitchen door and straight over to the fridge.

"I thought you were taking the night off."

"I kept watch over Al and Mary."

My eyes opened wide. "Is there a new threat?"

"Only if someone other than us has their eyes on you."

"And?"

Diesel looked at his phone's screen. "We're clear."

I was relieved, given there was no way I wanted to put the brakes on this burgeoning thing with Maisie. If there had been a threat, I would be forced to.

"She's stopping by tomorrow for lunch." The only person who looked as though he'd heard me was my brother.

"Need me to make myself scarce?"

"As long as you and Onyx plan to work next door, I don't think it's necessary." I took another look around the room. "Where is he, anyway?"

"Called it an early night. I think the cold weather is exacerbating his pain."

The man had been shot twice at point-blank range along with surviving a plane crash. If anyone deserved to lay low and nurse his aches and pains, it was our boss.

I downed the rest of the beer in the bottle I'd opened when I came inside. "I think I'll call it a night myself."

"Yep, you need all the beauty sleep you can get. Maisie's gonna see you in the daylight tomorrow."

"Fuck off," I muttered to Jimmy, tossing the bottle in the recycle bin and taking the stairs two at a time.

I stripped down without turning the lights on and walked over to the window where I could see the second story of Al and Mary's camp. If it didn't make me a fucking creeper, I would've picked up my binoculars to see if Maisie had left her window shade open. Instead, I turned the water on in the shower, knowing damn well I'd never get to sleep unless I took the edge off.

4

Maisie

I flopped on the bed for the second time in the last few hours, forgetting how much noise the creaky bedsprings made. I stilled, listening to see if either of my grandparents would say anything. They didn't.

I got up and unbuttoned my dress, letting it fall to the floor as I pretended Ranger was watching. I unclasped my bra, let it fall too, and pressed my full breasts together, wishing his fingers were pinching my nipples rather than my own. I slid my panties off my hips and crawled between the ice-cold sheets of my bed. Even that did nothing to cool the heat between my legs.

Ranger Messick was the hottest, sexiest, most fuckable man I'd ever known, and I had no intention of letting much more time go by without knowing how he felt sunk deep inside me.

I replayed every sexy innuendo, every playful touch, every kiss, every sweep of his tongue as I gave myself the release I knew I'd need to get any sleep.

Still, I tossed and turned most of the night, finally deciding at dawn to just get out of bed and start my day. If I kept myself busy enough, maybe time wouldn't drag between now and noon.

My first order of business was to finalize getting the insurance that would allow us to open the dance hall on the weekends. Since I'd been able to get a special event policy for New Year's Eve, I didn't anticipate having a problem converting it to full coverage. Thankfully, it went as smoothly as I'd hoped.

I knew it would be nowhere near as easy once it came to insuring the rides on the midway, but that was a fight for another day.

I smiled when, at eleven thirty, my cell phone rang with a call from Ranger.

"I was just getting ready to head your way. I hope we're still on for lunch today."

He laughed. "Remember last night when I asked if you could make it thirteen hours?"

"Of course I do."

"Well, I'm the one who's run out of patience. I've been counting the minutes since I woke up this morning. I probably shouldn't tell you that."

"Why not?"

"I don't know. Aren't guys supposed to play hard to get or something?"

"No. That was women in the fifties. These days, playing hard to get is a definite turnoff."

"Does that mean you're turned on, Maisie?"

"I have been since last night, haven't you?"

"Oh, yeah."

I lowered my voice to a whisper. "To be perfectly honest, I had to do something about it before I could fall asleep."

I heard a crash that sounded like the phone hitting the floor followed by a bunch of rustling.

"Everything okay?"

"Yeah, fine. The boner you just gave me knocked the phone out of my hand."

I couldn't help it; I laughed out loud.

"Sure, you think it's funny. Just wait until I get you back."

"I can assure you, I'm waiting with bated breath."

"Damn, girl. Get that sweet ass—along with the rest of your delectable body—over here."

"Should I bother bringing the leftovers?"

"Damn straight. We're both going to need some nourishment for what I have planned the rest of the day."

By four in the afternoon, I was ready to rip my clothes off and demand Ranger touch me—anywhere—I didn't care where. Either that, or I'd combust.

The man played cat and mouse with me since I'd arrived. First by insisting we eat. When we finished, he invited me next door, to see the progress his brother and Onyx were making on Blanca's camp. After that, he suggested we take a drive over to the boarded-up Canada Lake Hotel so he could see how much of an investment I thought it would take to turn it into a "destination resort."

I might've thought he'd lost interest in me if it weren't for the way he brushed his body against mine whenever he walked past me. Or how he leaned in every so often and whispered, "Anything I can do for you, Maisie Ann?"

When he drove up to his camp and came around to open my door, I was ready for him. He held out his hand, but rather than taking it, I put mine on his shoulder and slid my way down his body until my feet hit the ground.

"I told my grandmother I'd be home in time to help her get dinner ready," I said, wriggling away from him when Ranger put his hands on my waist. "Have a good night, and thanks for today. It was…fun."

Evidently, I'd stunned him since when I looked over my shoulder, he was still standing in the same place, eyes wide, mouth open.

"Hold up," I heard him holler when I got to my car and opened the door. He jogged over to me. "I thought we were going to hang out longer."

I looked at my watch. "I'd say four hours is the longest lunch I've ever taken."

"What about after dinner? We could—"

"Sounds good. Why don't you come over around seven?" I slid into the driver's seat much in the same way I'd slid down his body. "See ya later, Ranger," I said with a wink, pulling my door closed.

As I drove off, I glanced in the rearview mirror. "Mission accomplished," I muttered to myself when I saw him standing where I'd left him, hands on his hips, eyes wide, and mouth open.

"Hello, sweetheart. How was your afternoon?" my grandmother asked when I came inside and took off my coat.

"Okay."

She raised a brow. "Just okay?"

"Not quite what I expected. So, what's for dinner?"

She motioned with her head in the direction of the slow cooker. "Chicken and dumplings."

I bit my bottom lip. "Anything I can help with? How about we have a salad with it?"

Her facial expression was almost as stunned as Ranger's.

"What?"

"A salad?"

Granted, it wasn't like me to suggest having one. Fortunately, my metabolism allowed me to eat pretty much whatever I wanted without worrying about gaining weight. On the other hand, I wasn't getting any younger. Maybe it was time for me to consider eating more vegetables or at least increasing my fiber intake.

"It'll be good for us," I mumbled, reaching into the crisper.

"Come sit with me," she said when I set the produce on the counter. "You seem out of sorts. Tell me what happened today."

"Nothing." And wasn't that the God's honest truth? While I hadn't expected we'd spend the afternoon messing up his sheets, I had certainly been looking forward to a kiss hello. At least. I blinked away the tears threatening to fill my eyes, making me feel like a fourteen-year-old all over again.

She put her hand on mine and squeezed my fingers. "Maisie?"

"I've had a crush on him for as long as I can remember."

"It seems the feeling is mutual."

"I thought so and then today…I don't know. It was different."

"Well, I can see how you might feel insecure. I mean, in the last forty-eight hours, Ranger has been to our house for dinner and spent the majority of that time in enraptured conversation with you. Then, last night, the two of you went out for dinner, after which you practically floated your way into the house and up the stairs, and finally, you spent this afternoon together. So, yes, I get it."

"He's just so…so…"

"Handsome," said my grandmother. "My word, the man could be a model." She fanned her face, stood, and got a glass of water.

Handsome wasn't the word I was going to use, but he certainly was. And so charming. Last night at dinner, I noticed he'd shaved the beard he sported the night before, making him look younger than me. Then today, the scruff had grown back, so he appeared more rugged.

His features with or without facial hair were as perfect as if they'd been sculpted, and in the years since I'd first been dumbstruck by his toned physique, his shoulders had broadened and his arms looked like they were twice the size. Imagining him naked made my heart pound and my palms sweat.

What about me, though? I hadn't worked out a day in my life. I was always active—that was what drove my metabolism—but I had zero muscle definition. Maybe I should consider joining a gym. The closest one was in Johnstown, though, and that was forty-five minutes from here. I made a mental note to add workout facilities to the list of amenities that would be necessary to make the Canada Lake Hotel destination-worthy. Along with a world-class spa, of course.

"I invited him over after dinner."

My grandmother smiled. "Let me guess. He accepted?"

I nodded. "I hope that's okay."

"This is your home, Maisie. You don't have to ask permission to invite your friends over. Besides, your granddad and I will be at Walt and Ida's for bridge tonight."

"I forgot." Great, now Ranger would think I invited him over so we could be alone. Maybe I should text and tell him something came up. Except he could see our camp from his place. He'd probably see my grandparents leave.

"Here. Drink this." My grandmother set a glass of sherry in front of me. "In fact, have two."

5

Ranger

"Where did Maisie run off to?" asked Jimmy when I joined him out on the porch.

"Said she promised to help Mary get dinner ready."

"But?"

"I think I screwed up." I told him how flirty we'd been and that I'd pulled back a little this afternoon. "It might've backfired."

Jimmy looked out at the lake and sighed. "Just be you, Range. You be you, and let Maisie be herself, and everything will go fine. When you start second-guessing each other is when the problems start."

"I was afraid I came off as overeager at dinner—especially afterwards."

"Did Maisie complain?"

"Nah. In fact, she said playing hard to get was a turnoff."

"And yet that's what you did."

"I didn't think she was gonna go home. I thought we'd have dinner together and, you know, hang out."

"When do you think you'll see her again?"

"Tonight. She invited me over after dinner."

"So you got your second chance. Don't fuck it up again."

I looked out at the lake like he had. "I really like her, man."

"No kidding. Here's the deal. From what I've seen, the feeling is mutual. Don't overthink shit. Just go with it."

"Got it."

"You gettin' hungry?" he asked.

"Yeah. What are you thinking?"

"Sandwiches from the Canada Lake Store? I'll buy if you fly."

"Who's flying?" asked Wasp, joining us out on the porch along with Swan.

"I'm off to pick up sandwiches for dinner. Want one?"

"I do," said Cowboy. "The one with roast beef."

"I'll take one of those too," said Diesel.

"Is there some kind of meeting going on here that I'm unaware of?" I asked when I saw Onyx and Buster walk in the kitchen door like the others had.

"I think we're all just bored," Diesel said, grabbing a beer from our fridge and holding it out to me. "Except you, that is."

"He thinks he screwed up with Maisie."

I glared at my brother.

"How so, son?" asked Onyx.

"I'd rather not go into it again, thanks."

Swan walked over and took the Canada Lake Store menu out of my hand. "What did you do?"

"He played hard to get," Jimmy answered for me.

"That only works for French women," she said absentmindedly. "I'll take one of the turkey sandwiches, please. No bread."

"No bread? How is it a sandwich, then, sis?" asked Onyx. Swan rolled her eyes and patted his stomach.

"Looks like you might want to skip the carbs too, my friend."

"Shit. Not only are we all bored, we're getting fat too."

Swan smacked him. "You may be, but I'm certainly not."

"Hey, you gonna let your lady hit me, bro?" Onyx said to Wasp. Based on the look he and Swan shot in our boss' direction, my guess was there was trouble in paradise for them too.

It took an hour for the lake store to get all the sandwiches we'd ordered made, and by then, Diesel, who'd gone with me, and I had downed our second beer and were sitting out on their front porch under the heat lamps.

"Hey, Ranger," said Mary, getting out of the car when Al pulled up near the steps. "I didn't expect to run into you here."

"Nor I, you." I leaned down and waved at Al.

"We're on our way to the Bancrofts for bridge, and we were out of beer to take with us."

"Sorry about that. We cleaned you out a couple of nights ago."

Diesel went to wait in the car while I followed her in, figuring the least I could do was buy her a couple of six-packs to make up for what my brother, Onyx, and I'd drank when we were over for dinner.

"You seem as out of sorts as Maisie is," she said, catching me rolling my shoulders.

My head shot up. "She's out of sorts?"

She patted my cheek. "I'll say this much; don't cancel on her tonight."

Cancel? Hell, I was thinking of showing up early. "I won't."

"Al and I will be out until eleven, at least. Unless we're winning. Then, it might be midnight," she added with a wink.

"Order for Ranger," I heard the girl behind the counter holler.

"That's me."

"Have a good time tonight!" Mary shouted after me.

"You too!"

After asking the girl at the register to add Mary's beer to my store tab, I carried the box of sandwiches out to my SUV, where Al stood waiting for me.

"Hello, sir. What can I do for you?" I asked.

"You can stop with the sir crap. You probably never knew this, but I rubbed whiskey on your gums when you were a baby to get you to stop crying."

I laughed. "I didn't know. Did it work?"

"Of course it worked. It was just fine for generations of teething babies. Nowadays, doing such a thing would get a fella thrown in jail."

"Somehow, I don't think you're standing by my truck just to tell me that."

"No, I'm not." He looked over at the store, maybe checking to see if Mary was on her way out. "You know Maisie is our only grandchild."

"I do."

"Some might say her parents were never very... parental, if you know what I mean."

I knew that too, but since it was from eavesdropping on my mother gossiping about it, I didn't say so.

"She's no worse for wear because of it since she had her grandma and me in her life. There are just times she isn't quite as sure of herself as you might expect her to be."

"I suffer from some of that myself."

Al raised a brow.

"At least where your granddaughter is concerned."

He shook his head and laughed. "You don't need advice from me, then. The two of you will figure it out." I could swear I heard him say, "Two damn peas in a pod," when he walked away.

"What was that all about?" asked Diesel, who'd been waiting in the SUV for me.

"Everyone has advice for Maisie and me."

"Advice? You went on one date. What the hell do you need advice about?"

"As I told my brother, I really like her."

Diesel shook his head. "You're a goddamn covert operative, Ranger. You've been on all the same missions I have, and never once have I seen you be a pussy. Don't start that shit now."

"I'm not. It's just that—"

"No, it's not *just* anything. Knock this crap off. You want Maisie? Go *get* her and quit fucking overthinking everything. *Got it*?"

"Got it."

"Thank God. I don't want to hear any more talk of you—"

"Then, quit talking about it."

"Shit. Sorry. You're right. I'm about to go after whoever put a hit out on the K19 team myself just because I'm so fucking bored."

I doubt I'd wolfed down another sandwich as fast as I did tonight. Three minutes from start to finish. Same with my shower. Another two to get dressed, and I was on my way out the door. Hell, I was a half hour early, but since I knew Al and Mary weren't home, I was following my best friend's advice. I wanted Maisie Ann Jones, and I was about to get her.

"Um, hi," she said, opening the door when I knocked.

"Can I come in?"

She stepped to the side. "Sure. Is everything okay?"

I shook my head as I closed the door behind me and crowded her against it.

"It's not?"

"Nope, but I'm about to make it that way." I lowered my head and kissed Maisie the same way I had in the truck last night, the same way I should've the minute I saw her this morning, and the way I should've all afternoon.

I leaned my body into hers and felt her nipples harden through the fabric of my shirt. And finally, I put my hands under her ass and lifted her so she could feel exactly how much I wanted her. I walked us over to the sofa and sat, holding her on my lap so I could keep kissing her as long as I wanted to or as long as she'd let me.

I devoured her lips, her tongue, her mouth, and all the while, my fingers were weaved in her hair so I could shift the angle of her head as it suited me.

The other thing it did was prevent me from touching any other part of her body because even though I ached for her, neither of us was ready for the intimacy of sex.

"Um, wow," she said, resting her head on my chest. I had no idea how long we'd been lip-locked at that point, and I didn't care. All I knew was the sun had long since set and I was nowhere near finished.

"I'm sorry I was such a jackass today," I whispered as I scattered kisses along her jawline.

"You definitely were, and you're also definitely forgiven."

Maisie raised her head and led our kiss, this time keeping her eyes wide open and focused on mine. I never kept track of how many women I'd made out with, but I could say for certain this was the first time both our eyes were open.

Rather than delving deep, Maisie slowly ran the tip of her tongue over both my lips before teasing me by touching it to the tip of mine. It was all I could do to keep myself from imagining how her mouth would feel when she used it on other parts of my body.

She leaned back and put the tip of her finger where her tongue had just been. "I have a proposition for you."

I raised both eyebrows. I was being as good a boy as I knew how, but if Maisie put sex on the table first, I had no idea how I'd be able to turn her down.

"I would love to know what you're thinking right now," she said, but since she hadn't moved her fingers from my lips, I remained quiet. "I need to do some market research, and in order to get my information firsthand, I want to visit some of the other higher-end hotels and spas in the park. Maybe a few outside of it too. I was wondering if you might like to help."

I wound my tongue around her fingers. "Give me those," I said, grabbing them when she trailed their wet tips down my neck, knowing exactly what would happen if I let her keep going. "I'd love to help. Just tell me how."

"Testing mattresses, evaluating couple's massages, that kind of thing. Oh, and food. That will be important too."

"I'm in." It was going to require some finagling on my part since, in essence, I wasn't supposed to travel outside a twenty-five-mile radius from my camp.

However, if I could clear it with Onyx and have a couple of the guys tail us, there was a chance the big bosses back at K19 Security Solutions would give me permission to travel a little farther away.

I scooted Maisie from my lap. "There are a couple of things we need to talk about first."

"Okay," she said, barely above a whisper. Her eyes were back to wide, and she bit her bottom lip.

"How much do you know about what I do for a living?"

"Probably more than you think I do. If it's true."

I cocked my head.

"C'mon, Ranger. There was a shootout at your camp a few weeks ago, and a medivac helicopter landed in the meadow. Shortly after that, more black SUVs with tinted windows showed up than I've ever seen outside of Washington, DC. If you think the entire county, maybe even the whole park, wasn't speculating on what happened, you're in the wrong business."

"You said, 'if it's true.' What did you mean by that?"

"You're actually going to make me say it?"

I smiled and nodded.

"You work for the government."

I laughed. "Which part?"

"The secret part."

"Use your words, Maisie."

"Okay, the CIA."

"Used to. And before you ask why I'm telling you, every single person who was here when that all went down has been thoroughly vetted. That includes you and your grandparents."

"What about my parents?"

"Them too."

"Even though they weren't here?"

"Even though."

The fact that I hadn't known Sherman's Amusement Park was named after an actual person in Maisie's family still bothered me, but it wasn't the kind of information that would've needed to be included in a background report.

"So, you know I'm not a spy," she said.

"I wouldn't say that necessarily. After all, your proposition will involve some reconnaissance." I brought her palm to my lips and kissed it. "I would very much like to go with you, but before I make any firm plans, I need to clear it with the people I work for."

She made a funny face. "Really?"

I made the same face she had. "Yes, and there's more."

"More?"

"If I am able to join you, we'll have company."

"Oh, um…"

"Not directly with us, but watching over us, so to speak."

"How much watching exactly?"

"Unless we're out in public, they won't know what we're wearing—or not wearing."

"Will they be able to hear us…you know…talking?"

I laughed out loud. "Only if I want them to." Maisie looked like she'd swallowed her tongue. "I'm kidding. No, they won't be able to hear us talking or, ahem… doing anything else."

"Are they watching us now?"

"They know I'm here. They're also making sure no one else is who shouldn't be."

"What about at dinner last night?"

"Yep. They were in the vicinity."

Maisie's cheeks turned pink. "Could they see us in your car?"

"Remember what I said about us being out in public?"

"Oh my God. I'm mortified." She tried to scoot away, but I pulled her back on my lap.

"Don't be. I'm sure they were aware of what was happening, but I doubt very much they watched."

"How long will it take before you know whether you can do this or not?"

"I should have an answer sometime tomorrow. When were you thinking of leaving?"

"As soon as you get your answer."

I smiled and nuzzled her neck. "I sure do like you, Maisie Ann Jones, and you're not the first person I've told today."

"Who else?"

"Both of your grandparents."

She groaned. "I was afraid you were going to say that."

"It isn't a bad thing, beautiful. Speaking of Al and Mary, what are they going to think about us going away together?"

"I'm twenty-six years old, Ranger, and I went to college. They aren't going to think a thing, except for my grandmother, who will be happy I finally stopped second-guessing you."

"I was doing plenty of that on my own."

She wrapped her arm around my neck and rested her head on my shoulder. "I was too. I mean about myself."

I put my finger on her chin. "Let's make an agreement not to do that anymore. At least not with each other."

"It isn't that easy. We hardly know each other."

"A few minutes ago, you said you know more about me than I think you do. Right back at ya, sweetheart."

"True, but those are things, facts, information. Not what makes you or me tick."

I brought my mouth to her ear and blew into it. "Finding out what makes you tick is going to be my favorite part," I whispered.

6

Maisie

Oh…My…God. We were really going to do this. If Ranger could get permission.

There was some risk involved. I meant what I said. We really didn't know each other, not the most important parts. I'd thought about that before I propositioned him, though.

At least at the first place we stayed, I'd reserve separate rooms. Next, we wouldn't spend more than two nights at any one place. That way, if things got weird between us, we'd go back to the lake and on our separate ways. Finally, even though I could write off the expenses of this trip, we'd split them down the middle so neither of us felt taken advantage of.

Ranger ran his finger down my cheek. "What's got you thinking so hard?"

"Rules."

His eyes opened wide. *"Rules?"*

"Parameters. Does that sound better?"

He laughed. "No."

"I just want to make sure we both have an out if we need one."

He shifted me off his lap and took both of my hands in his. "Look, I know it seems like things are moving really fast between us, but I can assure you I would never intentionally do anything to make you uncomfortable. If I do, I want you to say so. *Immediately.* Understood?"

"And vice versa?"

"I doubt you could ever make me uncomfortable, but sure. If you do, I'll say so."

"Can I ask you something?"

"Pretty sure we've already established you can."

I smiled when he winked. "Have you ever been in a serious relationship?"

"No."

His answer was so quick and so emphatic, it took me by surprise.

"And before you say anything else, unless you haven't been either, I don't want to know about it."

"I haven't, but why wouldn't you want to know if I had been?" I asked.

"I told you that if you hadn't been leaving for college the day after your birthday party, I would've claimed you as my own, Maisie. The idea that anyone else did before I could, makes me a little crazy."

"Um…I'm not a virgin, Ranger."

"Okay, but you said you weren't in a serious relationship before, so that means whoever you may have had sex with isn't someone who mattered." He shuddered. "Not that it's something I want to think about."

"Okay, well, I didn't want you to get the wrong impression. I *have* had sex before."

"Not talking about it, remember?"

"I doubt you're a virgin."

"I'm not, but I don't want to talk about that either."

While I was tempted to roll my eyes, I actually found his intransigence kind of cute. "So we don't talk about anything—you know, like, sexual stuff—that happened before."

Ranger shook his head. "I consider kissing to be 'sexual stuff,' and I'm all for talking about the first time we spent a couple of hours doing that. In fact, if I remember right, it went something like this."

He captured my face between his hands and crushed his mouth to mine. Yep, that was exactly the way I remembered it too.

It was a little after three the next day before I heard from Ranger again after we said good night shortly after my grandparents got home from their bridge game.

"Pack your bags," he said when I answered his call.

"Yeah? I'm excited you can go."

"I should've asked you this last night, but where are we headed?"

"I thought we'd start somewhere relatively close, but that leaves several places we can check out."

"Hmm. Relatively close. Let me try to guess. Saratoga Springs?"

"How did you know?"

"Well, outside of Lake Placid and maybe Lake George, I can't think of anywhere else that would have *several* places we can check out."

And therein lay the biggest problem I faced with trying to bring Canada Lake back to what it was in its heyday. Back then, there were at least two dozen other lakes in the region that were just as much of a destination as this had been. Now, there were two because, like he said, Lake George didn't really count.

"Next question. What time are we leaving?"

I laughed. "Shouldn't we decide which day first?" Ranger didn't respond, so I thought maybe the call had dropped. "Hello?"

"I'm here."

He sounded like a dejected little boy. "What's wrong?"

"You said we could leave as soon as I got my answer."

"Oh my gosh. I wasn't serious. We have to make reservations and decide what restaurants we want to try and stuff like that."

"Can't we do that from there?"

"I guess so, but we will have to make room reservations."

"Tell me where, and I'll handle it."

"Um, that's okay. I can, uh, do it."

"Maisie? Think about this for a minute. I'll need to make more than one set of reservations, at least for where we stay."

"Oh…Right…Well…Um…"

"Spit it out."

I lowered my voice, looking around to see if either of my grandparents were in the vicinity. Especially my grandma. "I was thinking that at first, we should probably get separate rooms."

"Thank you for telling me. We can absolutely do that."

"You won't mind?"

"Last night, I said I wanted you to tell me immediately if I did or said something to make you uncomfortable. Sharing a room is the perfect example. You aren't ready for that, and I understand."

"You aren't disappointed?"

"To be honest with you, I wouldn't have assumed we'd be sharing one tonight."

I could hardly tell him I was disappointed when I'd just told him it was what I wanted, but I was.

"Maisie? So. Separate rooms. How about… the Saratoga Arms? They have a full spa, choice of restaurants, and they've been in business for over one hundred years."

Even though he couldn't see me, I raised my eyebrows. "You're going to be good at this."

He groaned.

"What made you do that?"

"I was about to say something that would make you uncomfortable."

"Go ahead."

"I can't now."

"Okay, let's backtrack. What did I say? Oh yes, I said you're going to be good at this. Go ahead. What were you going to say?"

"I can't now," he repeated.

"If you say it, I'll agree to leave tonight instead of waiting until tomorrow."

He cleared his throat. "I plan to be good at everything where you're concerned, beautiful. Damn good."

"I'll be ready to leave in a half hour."

I'd laid everything out on my bed earlier in the day, so I could've been ready in five minutes. I wanted to take another shower first, though, and put on enough makeup that I looked good but didn't appear to be wearing any. Then there was the matter of what to wear. It would take me just as long to decide what to wear underneath—because honestly, did I really think I could resist spending the night in Ranger's arms? Especially after that hotter-than-all-get-out make-out session last night.

"Knock, knock."

"Come in, Grandma." I looked over my shoulder at her. "What's up?"

She walked over to the bed where my suitcase lay open and tucked a plastic bag under a layer of clothes.

"What's that?"

She patted my cheek. "I wasn't sure if you had time to get to a drugstore, so I picked you up a little box of something for your trip."

"Grandma!" I gasped, pulling out the bag and peeking inside at the box of condoms. She took it from my hand and put it back in the suitcase.

"Just in case, sweetheart."

"I could probably equally use a bottle of sherry."

"I can go get a bottle from the pantry."

I put my hand on her arm. "I'm kidding. I'm sure they serve it wherever Ranger has chosen for us to have dinner tonight."

"It always makes a nice aperitif. Especially in the winter."

I put my arms around her. "Thank you."

"You're welcome, dear. I take it things worked out okay last night?"

"We talked."

She raised a brow.

"Oh my God. I'm not having this conversation with you."

"Don't be such a prude, Maisie. I learned about the birds and the bees when I was younger than you are now."

"Like I said. Not having this conversation."

She rolled her eyes. "All right, then. When do you think you'll be back?"

"Probably the day after tomorrow, but I'll let you know if that changes."

"I hope you have fun, sweetheart. Ranger is a good man, and the two of you are well suited."

"We're just going away for a couple of days. We aren't eloping."

"Stranger things have happened." She winked and left the room.

"Where's our company?" I asked when Ranger put my bag in the back of his SUV after we said goodbye to my grandparents.

"They're around. It's doubtful you'll notice them as long as they do their job correctly."

"My grandmother gave me a box of condoms," I blurted after we were in the SUV and on our way to the highway.

Ranger coughed. "Um, I see."

"I didn't want you to think I went out and bought them."

"Much better if I imagine her doing it."

"It could be worse. Al could've been the one to get them."

He cringed. "Yeah, that mental picture is definitely worse." He reached over and wrapped my hand in his. "I don't want you to think I was being presumptuous, but I brought some too."

"We're both being presumptuous, Ranger. I mean, do you really think there's a chance we won't have sex?"

7

Ranger

Obviously, I assumed we would, given we couldn't keep our hands off each other. What I wasn't sure of was whether it would be tonight.

All the unsolicited advice I'd been given raced through my head, none more so than Diesel's.

"I'm trying not to overthink anything," I finally said. "Just let things happen."

"I'm all for that."

We drove in silence a few more minutes, but I had something I wanted to say. Rather than "second-guess" myself again, I went for it. "You asked me if I'd ever been in a serious relationship before."

"You said you hadn't."

"That's right, but I didn't say why." I glanced over at her, and she'd turned her body so she was facing me. "I could blame it on the work I do, which would have made it difficult if I'd ever wanted to. Be in a serious relationship, that is."

"I'm following."

"I never met anyone who interested me that much."

"Me neither. I dated in college, but no one really took."

I could feel myself cringe, and it was worse when she laughed.

"Oh my God, are you really that insecure?"

I thought about the question for a minute. "Insecure? No. Not at all. In fact, it's probably the opposite."

"You have a lot to be secure about."

I smiled. "I'll be happy to circle back to that later, but I want to finish this part of the conversation first."

She nodded.

"I never considered myself to be the jealous type, but I can't even *think* about someone else having his hands on you." I shook my head and looked out the window into the darkness. "I'm turning into a caveman."

Maisie giggled. "I kind of like it."

"Yeah, well, I don't." I flexed both my hands. "So anyway, back to relationships, or my lack of them. I told you last night that I really like you, Maisie. I meant it."

"I really like you too."

"We're in agreement, then. So…I say we just let this thing between us go wherever it's supposed to."

"I'm in."

"Which means that after we check into the Saratoga Arms, I'll be putting both of our bags in the same room. Then, dinner."

"Still in."

I'd been paying attention when she went through her list of things she'd need my help with. Mattress checks were settled, and tomorrow morning, she'd be in for a couple of surprises before we even left our room.

Since neither of us was dressed for a fancier venue and changing our clothes might have meant we wouldn't leave the room again, we opted for the most casual of the Arms' restaurants.

"This is exactly what I'm talking about," Maisie said as she perused the menu. "Everything sounds so good, and it's all so different from the usual pub food."

"I was thinking we could pick a few things to share."

Her face broke into a smile, and she did a little dance in her chair. "I love that idea."

"You pick first."

She tapped her lips with her finger. "I'm between the crawfish beignets and the garlic-butter baked oysters for an appetizer."

"I vote for both. And for dinner, the lamb and grass-fed-beef burger with bacon and blue cheese, and the buttermilk fried chicken."

"They only have two desserts, so both?"

"And a bottle of Prosecco to start?"

She swooned. "I'm pretty sure I've died and gone to heaven."

I leaned forward and curled my finger so she'd come closer. "That comes later, beautiful. For both of us."

"Tell me what you think works about Saratoga Springs as a destination area," I asked after we'd ordered and were enjoying the first few sips of wine.

Maisie laughed. "Everything." She looked around the crowded room. "It's only an hour from Canada Lake, and yet they're worlds apart."

I had to agree. "Is there a way to find out where all these people are traveling from?"

"As a matter of fact, I have a friend at the chamber of commerce who said she'd be willing to share the information she has. When I told her about my plans, she agreed that whatever we do will only benefit the entire region. Also, you do know Saratoga Springs isn't actually within the state park boundaries?"

I'd noticed when we were on our way here but hadn't thought much about it. It wasn't like there was an entrance fee for people to pay like there was for national parks. "Does that make a difference?"

"Sales tax is a couple of cents higher, and property tax rates in New York State are among the highest in the country, which makes it harder on any business, especially mom-and-pop types."

"You said you were going to start this revitalization campaign by bringing the amusement park back. What do you need to make that happen?" While it was already established that I wasn't exactly good with things like hammering nails or cutting wood, there were other ways I could help. Financially, in particular.

"It's a conundrum, honestly. In order to bring the amusement park back, we need more people to come to the lake. In order for more people to come to the lake, we need to make it a destination. One of the issues we're facing is the lack of lodging. There is ten times the number of vacation rentals on other lakes compared to Canada Lake. At least."

I knew from being there last summer that many of the camps sat empty for most of it. "That should be a fairly easy fix. What keeps someone from listing their property on one of those vacation-rental websites?"

Maisie shrugged. "How to do it? Managing it too, probably."

"There must be companies that do that."

A smile spread across Maisie's gorgeous face. "Are you really this into it, or are you just humoring me?"

I laughed. "I may be more into it than you are." At least until the Shadow Ops team got word that we could get back to business, this was something I could sink my teeth into. Diesel too, if it was okay with her.

"I have a colleague who might like to lend a hand."

"The more, the merrier. I'll take all the help I can get."

"I have a personal question to ask you."

She raised a brow. "Just one?"

"I know you said you were looking for investors for the hotel, but what about with the amusement park? What kind of investment will that require?"

"That isn't terribly personal. I mean, as far as Sherman's goes, it's never been in debt. Grandpa Jones paid for everything in cash in those days. Although, I do anticipate the insurance costs to get the midway open will be astronomical."

"And how are you fixed for funds?"

"Ah, there's the personal question. I would think that if you've 'thoroughly vetted' our family, you'd already know the answer."

"Financials are need-to-know."

She raised a brow. "Interesting. Well, to answer your question, I can do some on my own, but not all. The question is how much personal money I want to invest. Then there's my parents and grandparents, but the same question pertains. They might not want to invest anything. Which means the more developer funds I can secure, the better."

"I may be interested in investing."

Maisie's eyes scrunched, and she studied me. "What we need is significant, outside of the amusement park." She shrugged. "Which may also be significant. I don't have exact figures yet."

"When you do, let's talk."

"Since you asked me, I'm going to ask you. I don't know a lot about your family's financial history, but do you…they…you, have the means?"

"This would be me, not my family, and the answer is yes. I have the means. Significant means."

"Next question."

I nodded.

"Why?"

"Several reasons. 'I grew up here' would be the most obvious. I remember what it was like when I was a kid. Not that it was anything compared to when my grandparents and great-grandparents hung out here." I perused the room. "Based on what I see here, and it being the off-season, the potential for Canada Lake is worth being a part of building it back."

She opened her mouth to say something, but stopped when I held up my hand.

"The less obvious would be that I believe in you, Maisie. Everything I've seen and heard tells me you do your research, you're prudent in your approach, and your thinking is sound."

"Wow." She sat back in her seat. "I hope I measure up."

I leaned forward, tracing my fingers over the back of her hand. "You will more than measure up, beautiful."

We spent the rest of dinner talking about some of the other things Maisie had in mind for the lake's redevelopment, which included a carousel museum along with an interactive visitor center that would allow tourists to be fully immersed into what the Adirondacks were like back when the first great camps were built in the late eighteen hundreds.

As our dinner began winding to an end, I noticed Maisie seemed increasingly nervous. I scooted my chair closer to hers and put my arm across the back of it. "We have two rooms reserved tonight for you and me. There is nothing to say we can't make use of both of them tonight."

She smiled. "Oh, yeah?"

I flexed the hand that was behind her back. "To sleep."

"It's just that dinner was very *business-y*."

"I kind of ruined the romantic vibe, didn't I?"

"We both did."

"Then, I say we call it a night and agree to meet up tomorrow morning." I'd have to check with the front desk to see if I could reschedule the surprise I'd arranged for her. If not, I'd just pay for it and book it again for the next day.

"I'm sorry."

"Hey, none of that. There isn't anything to be sorry for. No one is leaving for college tomorrow, remember? We're in no hurry."

She shrugged, but I could sense her worry and maybe even disappointment.

"It's early. Let's take a walk before we end our evening." While not a lot of Christmas decorations remained, I'd noticed the grounds of the Saratoga Arms were still lit up with white twinkle lights.

"I'd like that."

"I'll go grab the jackets we left in the room and meet you back here."

"I'll use the ladies' room."

Before Maisie and I separated in the lobby, I wrapped my arms around her. "I like being with you. It doesn't matter what we're doing. I can honestly say I've rarely been as engaged as I am with you." I leaned down and kissed her soft lips. "When the time is right, and not before, we'll share sheets. Okay?"

8

Maisie

I felt like an idiot, but I couldn't stand the idea of things feeling forced between Ranger and me. So far, everything that had happened, from dinner to kissing to talking about my plans for the lake, felt so natural.

I wanted the first time we had sex to feel the same way, not like we both expected it to happen so it had to. Maybe I was a romantic sap and he thought I was being silly, but that only made it worse.

Plus—God—that body. Even when he was asking me about investing, I had a hard time concentrating on anything besides the way his muscular chest looked like it was ridged beneath his shirt. Only after forcing myself to look at his face and nothing but his face, could I focus.

I watched him walk to the elevator, admiring the way his ass filled his jeans so perfectly and wondering what in the world I'd been thinking when I took sex off the table for tonight.

It could still happen, though. Right?

I shook my head. No. It couldn't. It wasn't fair to keep giving Ranger mixed signals, especially after saying we were just going to go with the flow and see where this thing took us.

I was still standing in the same place when the elevator opened and he walked in my direction, coats in hand.

"Ready?" he asked, lifting my jacket so I could ease my arms into it. I couldn't help but think of the first time he'd held my coat and told me how good I smelled. I peeked over my shoulder and caught him with his eyes closed, taking a deep breath, and giggled.

"You smell so damn good," he whispered, opening his eyes and catching me watching.

"So do you."

He sighed and took my hand. "Let's go check out the grounds. They're important, right?"

"Absolutely. The gardens here are spectacular. That's another thing the hotel should offer—weddings."

"Another great idea."

I laughed. "Maybe it isn't. My grandmother is a big proponent of eloping."

"Yeah? Did she have anyone in mind when she made the suggestion?"

Why had I even said that? "I didn't say she suggested it. She's just a fan. They ran off and got married a couple of days after Grandpa Al proposed, rather than 'spend all that money.' I can't tell you how many times I've heard about the 'astronomical' amount of money my mother spent when she and my dad got married."

"Most of the weddings I've been to have been fairly simple." He rolled his eyes. "Except Jimmy's."

"I remember hearing about it."

"Hey, look!" I raised my head and followed Ranger's gaze to an outdoor ice rink. "Are you up for it?"

"Of course! If you are."

He bought tickets, and we sat down to put on our rental skates. "We have about an hour before they close."

"As many years as it's been since I've skated, that's probably more time than I'll need."

He nodded but didn't comment. Either he'd never been on skates, or he was born on them.

"You're an expert skater, aren't you?"

"It's been a couple of years, but I did play hockey."

"Figures."

He stopped lacing his skates and looked over at me. "What makes you say that?"

"Football, baseball, basketball. It only stands to reason you've played hockey too."

"You're right. I did play all those sports."

"And I watched." Another thing I probably shouldn't have admitted, but it was the truth.

He looked stunned. "You did?"

I laughed. "It's really disheartening to think of how many games I went to and you had no idea I was there."

"I wouldn't have been able to tell you a single person who was. At least back then. I didn't have surgery for my nearsightedness until after I left for college."

"I don't remember you wearing glasses."

"I didn't. Contacts. Which is why I couldn't see during games. Fortunately, I played offensive line in football, so I didn't have to see the ball thrown at me."

"And shortstop in baseball."

"That's right."

"I told you. Every game."

"Wait. You said games. It was *every* game?"

I wasn't the only one either. The stands were filled with Ranger Messick fans. "All the home ones anyway. Some of the away games." Thinking back on it, the girls from my class should have carpooled. Or rented a bus to save on gas.

He held out his hand and helped me onto the ice. Thankfully, I picked up on it as if I'd skated yesterday.

"Look at you. You're a pro," Ranger said, skating backwards but in front of me. "I love seeing your smile." He pulled out his phone, swiped the screen, and held it up. I smiled, then stuck my tongue out.

"How many photos are you taking?" I asked when he continued to hold it trained on me.

"I'm not. It's a video."

"Stop," I said, putting my hands in front of my face. He slowed and put his hand on my wrist.

"Please let me see you, Maisie. You take my breath away."

I lowered my hands, skated toward him, and wrapped one arm around his neck. He stuck his phone in his pocket and kissed me.

We skated the full hour, laughing, kissing, showing off the entire time. My cheeks hurt from smiling so much. "Thank you for that," I said as we were taking our skates off to turn them back in. "It was a lot of fun."

"I'm thinking the Canada Lake Hotel definitely needs an ice rink. Better yet, let's get one built in town. It could host all kinds of hockey tournaments—club teams, high school, even college teams."

I watched his face grow more animated the longer he talked about it. His enthusiasm was infectious, and it made me want to pick up the pace of my plans. I had to admit I lost faith that I'd even get Sherman's back in business plenty of times.

We held hands as we walked back to the hotel. When we passed an empty alcove seating area with a roaring fire in the pit, I led him to it.

"Mmm, I like this," he said when I pushed him down on the outdoor sofa and sat on his lap.

Kissing him was the same as it had been the first night in his truck—heady and full of the desire I felt almost every moment I was with him. Until tonight's dinner, when I felt like we'd transitioned into business associates.

I moaned when I felt his hand on my waist move up so his index finger brushed my nipple.

"Is this okay?" he asked, moving the other hand up as well.

"More than okay."

He turned our bodies so I was shielded from anyone walking past and put his whole hand over my breast, kneading my flesh. He kissed his way from my lips down my neck.

"Ranger…"

"Yeah, beautiful?"

"Take me to our room."

"Are you sure?"

"Either that, or I'll start removing clothes right here. I'm thinking we should start with yours."

9

Ranger

I stood with Maisie in my arms and carried her toward the hotel's lobby, my lips on hers the entire way. Inside, she'd have to walk directly in front of me to hide the steel-hard erection I had no chance of taming. I could still feel her nipple pressing into my palm even though I'd taken my hand off her breast minutes ago.

When we reached the lobby entrance, I set her on her feet, turned her so her back was to me, and put my hands on her shoulders. "Stay in front of me until we get to the elevator."

She giggled but did as I asked. Once inside with the door closed, I pressed her up against the back wall. She lifted her legs and wrapped them around my waist at the same time her arms went around my neck.

"Do you have any idea how much I want you?"

She raised a brow. "It's pretty evident."

I rested my forehead against hers. "Are you sure about this?"

Maisie cupped my cheek. "I'm sorry about earlier. Or I'm sorry about now. I know I'm sending mixed messages."

"Don't be sorry. Just be sure."

"I want you too. So much it hurts." She motioned with her head to the elevator panel. "We should probably hit one of those buttons."

I reached behind me without letting her slide to the ground and pressed our floor number. When it dinged and the door opened, I carried her to the room where I'd left our bags. She didn't know it, but it was *her* room. Only because I couldn't reach the key card with her in my arms, I let go.

I felt every inch of her body slide against mine while I fumbled with trying to get the card into the slot the right way.

She reached around and grabbed my ass. "You have the sweetest butt," she said, squeezing. "And it's so hard. Who knew an ass could have so much muscle?"

"Shh," I whispered when I heard the elevator ding again at the same time the room door finally clicked, indicating I'd gotten the card in correctly.

I got my mouth back on hers as fast as I could and my fingers woven into her hair so she couldn't break away from me until I was ready.

I loved kissing this woman. If how good her mouth felt was any indication of how sex would be between us, our bodies were made for each other.

I moved one hand from her hair, sneaking it under her sweater so I could feel the weight of her breast's fullness in my hand. "You have the greatest tits. I need to taste them."

Maisie pulled her sweater over her head. "The clasp is in front."

I unhooked it, walked backward to the bed, and positioned her between my legs. "God, Maisie. You are so fucking sexy." I squeezed her two mounds together so I could get both nipples in my mouth at the same time while she shrugged the bra from her shoulders.

"Ranger," she groaned.

"What, beautiful? Tell me what you need."

"You. Naked."

"Don't move." I reached behind me, pulled my shirt over my head, and threw it on the floor. I unfastened the clasp on her jeans and slowly lowered the zipper.

I toyed with leaving her panties on, but the thought of Maisie completely naked was more than I could wait for. "Take those off," I said once I'd pushed her jeans and underwear to her knees.

She stepped out of one side, and I couldn't wait. The second her legs were open, I thrust a finger into her tight, wet heat and leaned forward to attack her clit with my tongue. She stepped out with the other foot and wove her fingers in my hair. The last thing I expected was for her to back away, but she did.

She knelt between my legs and put her hands on the waistband of my jeans. "These off," she said, using the same demanding tone I had with her.

"Pull, darlin'." When she did, the buttons on my 501s released and my raging hard cock sprung out.

She leaned forward to lick the tip, but I stopped her. "Not yet."

She gave a little whimper when I pulled her to her feet and spun the two of us around. I eased her onto the bed and followed, nudging her knees open.

Her eyes met mine, and she put her hand in the middle of my chest. "Condom."

"Right." I turned to where I'd tossed my jeans and pulled out my wallet. "Don't worry, I have more," I said when she raised her eyebrows.

"Put it on."

"Needy little thing, aren't you?"

"You have no idea how long I've fantasized about this, Ranger." She eyed my cock. "I'm thrilled to say reality is even better."

I lined myself up with her pussy and slowly eased my way inside. I stopped and studied her. She was so tight. I didn't want to hurt her.

"More," she begged.

I went slow again, letting her body adjust to my size.

"Please, Ranger, give it all to me."

I did. One thrust and I was fully seated. My body trembled as I tried to hold myself back, but Maisie would have none of it. She wrapped her legs around me and shimmied her hips. When her pussy squeezed me, I couldn't hold back. I pushed into her a couple of times, then forced myself to still.

"Tell me what you fantasized about."

"Your hands, your mouth, all over my body."

"Believe me, beautiful, we're going to get there. Every fantasy you've ever had, I'm going to make come true."

"Please don't stop," she begged when I started to slowly move again. I snaked my hand between her legs and circled her clit with the tip of my finger.

"I want to watch you come, Maisie." I punctuated my words with deep thrusts and bored my eyes into hers. "Say my name."

"God, Ranger, I'm right there, *please*."

I pinched her clit, and she cried out, shattering in my arms. The look on her face, one I hoped I'd see a thousand times more in the course of my life, pushed me over the edge. As I let myself go, Maisie grabbed the back of my neck and pulled me into a kiss.

As much as I wanted to roar through my climax, her lips, her tongue on mine, turned it into the best orgasm I'd ever had.

"That was…I don't have words." I fell back on the bed, and Maisie climbed on top of me.

"I have one word."

"Yeah? Amazing? Incredible? Unbelievable?"

She shook her head. "More."

I put my arms around her and drew her body into mine. "Maisie Ann Jones, you are all my dreams come true."

"Yeah? Well, you're mine too."

"Wait. Where are you going?" I said when she climbed off me.

"More condoms." She unzipped her suitcase and pulled out a package. "Never thought I'd say this while naked with a boy in my bed, but thank goodness for Grandma Mary."

I growled when I pulled her back over me. "Not a naked boy. Me. You never thought you'd say that while you were naked in bed with Ranger Messick."

She giggled. "That's right. Naked with *Owen* Messick."

"Even better."

"Go away," Maisie groaned when a knock at the door woke us the next morning. After a night of very little sleep, spent making love, I was tempted to pull the pillow over my head too. However, two surprises awaited the woman whose body was probably as sore as mine.

"Coming," I hollered, getting out of bed and grabbing my jeans.

"What? No! Get back in bed," Maisie pleaded.

Before answering, I leaned over and kissed her. "It's worth it. I promise."

She pulled the blankets over her head.

I cracked the door open and took the breakfast tray from the room service guy. I'd made arrangements the day before to have it billed to my room and for the tip to be added. I made a mental note to discuss that with Maisie later. It was a service the Canada Lake Hotel should offer their guests too. I'd hate to have to sign a check now, half naked and trying to juggle a tray that held hot coffee.

"Thank you, sir," the guy said as I closed the door with my foot.

As I rounded the corner to the bed, Maisie moved the covers from her face. "Is that *coffee*?"

"I told you it was worth it."

When she sat up, the sheet fell, exposing her breasts, and the slight chill of the room hardened her nipples. I set the breakfast tray on the desk, dropped my jeans, and climbed on top of her. She broke out in a fit of giggles.

"My beard. Your poor skin," I muttered, running my fingertips over the red marks marring its otherwise flawlessness.

"I'll forgive you if you pour me a cup of coffee. God, it smells so good."

When I got up, I checked the time on my phone. We had two hours before her next surprise showed up.

"How do you take your coffee, beautiful?"

"I can get it. I was kidding when I asked you to."

"You can pour tomorrow."

She got out of bed anyway, walked over, and put her arms around my waist. I loved the feel of her naked body plastered against the back of mine. "Just some cream please." She peeked around me. "Wow, look at all that yumminess. Fruit and croissants. I didn't order this, did you?"

"I have to confess I did."

"It would be something if they included it with the room instead of the usual continental crap most places tout as breakfast. The cost, though." She made a plate, set it on the nightstand, and went into the bathroom. When she came out, she was wearing a robe and handed one to me. "Do you have any ideas what you'd like to do today?"

"I have a couple," I answered, winking as I took a bite of buttery croissant. "What about you?"

"I'd like to check out some of the other hotels, then later this afternoon, I have a meeting with my friend from the chamber of commerce."

"Do you want to stay here again tonight?"

Her eyes opened wide. "Do you want to go back to the lake?"

I laughed. "Not at all. I'd be happy extending our road trip. I thought maybe you'd like to compare some of the other lodging and their amenities."

"Do you mean it?"

"Which part? Extending our road trip? Absolutely. I'm in no hurry to get back to the place where you sleep in one camp and I sleep in another."

"Not tired of me?"

I pulled her into my arms. "I know this sounds crazy, but I can't imagine ever getting tired of being with you."

She reached up and kissed me. "I feel the same."

"Okay, so where to after this?"

While we ate, we mapped out which lakes we wanted to visit for a couple of hours and where we wanted to stay overnight. Maisie called her grandparents to let them know we'd be gone a few more days while I filled the two-person bathtub for us to soak in.

"This is the life," she said, nestling herself between my legs in the warm bath. "That's one problem with our camp. The bathrooms are entirely utilitarian."

"At least we don't have to use outhouses."

She laughed. "My grandfather tore ours down before I was born."

I moved her hair over one shoulder, covered her breasts with my palms, and kissed the side of her neck. "I planned something else for us this morning."

"You planned it?" She covered my hands with hers and squeezed.

"Turn around and straddle me." I helped her up and to turn around. Instead of on my lap, I positioned her on my thighs. "I like having access to these," I said, taking turns with her nipples before reaching around to cup the cheeks of her luscious ass.

"Ranger," she mewled, stroking my cock. "I need you inside me."

I groaned, wanting the same thing. "Condoms are in the other room."

"I'm on birth control." She bit her lip. "And I haven't been with anyone in longer than I want to admit."

It was the same for me. In fact, it had been so long, I couldn't remember the last time I'd been with a woman. "I've never had sex without a condom."

"Okay." She let go of my cock and slid back like she was getting up.

"Get back here." I grabbed her waist and shimmied her forward. "I've never had sex without a condom *until now*. Until you."

"You're sure?"

"I am if you are."

I lifted her up. My cock was hard enough that when she positioned her pussy at its tip and lowered herself on me, I was buried to the hilt in her heat. Skin on skin felt like nothing I'd ever known. The pleasure was almost too intense. I gripped her waist, slowing her movement. "Kiss me, Maisie."

I let her control the urgency of her mouth on mine in the same way I let her set the pace of her pussy on my cock. "God, woman," I groaned when she rose up enough that only my tip was inside her, then sunk all the way back down.

Her tits bounced as she started to move faster. She threw her head back and held onto the sides of the tub. When I felt her clench, heard her whimpers of pleasure, I put my hands on her ass and thrust with my hips.

"Come on, beautiful. Open your eyes and look at me."

She gasped and groaned my name, stilling as I felt her walls tighten around me.

"That's it, sweetheart." I slowly built our pace until I couldn't hold back any longer. I came inside her body, the first time in my life without the protection of a condom. Nothing had ever felt so good or so right. I'd never forget this moment no matter how long I lived, and I didn't want it to end. "Don't move. Stay right where you are."

She rested her cheek against my chest. "It's so good, right?"

"Good? No. It's the best sex I've had in my life."

"Me too."

We stayed that way, our bodies still joined together, until the water began to cool. I opened my mouth to tell her about her next surprise, when Maisie shifted off me.

"I need sustenance if we're going to keep at this."

"There are towels in the warmer." I pointed to the other side of the bathroom.

Her eyes opened wide. "Seriously? God, we have to do all of this." She took one out, wrapped it around her, and bit her lip. "It's going to cost a fortune."

While most of my focus had been on Maisie and her wonderland of a naked body, in the back of my mind, I kept thinking about her plans for the community that meant so much to both of us. I was in a position to make at least some of it happen. As much as I wanted to see her warm smile every day, I also believed she was onto something worth pursuing.

We'd just finished off the last of our breakfast when there was another knock at the door.

"Wow. Great timing. Is that lunch?"

"Um, not quite, but something I hope you'll find equally enjoyable."

Maisie sat back against the pillows and put her hands behind her head. "Nothing but enjoyment when I'm with you, Ranger."

"That's what I like to hear."

"Do I need to do anything?" she asked when I tightened the sash on my robe.

"Get ready to relax."

"Oh my God. You didn't?"

"I did," I said over my shoulder at the same time I opened the door to let the two massage therapists in who'd arrived for our appointment. I had booked a man and a woman, but the Neanderthal in me spoke up when I saw the guy they sent. No way in hell was he getting his hands on Maisie.

"Do you have a preference as to—"

I pointed to the female. "You for her."

Maisie giggled, got off the bed, and wrapped her arms around me. "I wouldn't have wanted *her* touching *you,* either."

They set up the tables, told us what to expect, and stepped out of the room. "I want to be able to touch you," I said when we were both facedown and I reached out between us. Maisie did the same, and we clasped hands.

"Thank you for this, Ranger."

"Market research, right?"

"I don't know about you, but I'm ready to stop thinking about business and start thinking about what we're going to do once our massages are over." She turned her head and winked.

"Great. Now I'm not going to be able to roll to my back through this whole thing."

10

Maisie

I was in a cocoon of happiness I never wanted to crawl out of. Ranger was sweet, smart, sexy, not to mention, the best-looking guy I'd ever been with. Actually, he was the best-looking guy I'd ever known.

When I was in high school, if anyone had told me that in only a few short years this is where I'd be and who I'd be with, I would've told them I had a better chance of winning the lottery.

We were partway through our massages and still hadn't dropped hands. I loved the feel of our fingers woven together and that we were still connected. I never wanted to let go. Not ever.

I knew exactly what he meant when he'd said he was in no hurry to get back to the place where I slept in one bed and he slept in another. After only one night, I already knew I'd miss him.

We'd decided to stay one more night here at the Saratoga Arms before heading up to Lake George for another two nights. I also needed to get to Lake Placid by the end of the week for a meeting with potential investors. I wasn't sure why I hadn't told Ranger about it. Wait. That wasn't true. I hadn't told him because one of the people who would be at the meeting was a man I'd had a relationship with when I was in college.

I'd been honest with him. It wasn't serious. In fact, the guy ended up being in another *relationship* at the same time he was dating me.

That I'd been duped left me feeling as humiliated as pissed. And while I really didn't want to face him ever again, he'd wheedled his way into the meeting when a mutual friend, whom we'd both attended Tuck with, let it slip it was taking place.

That he was so slimly and smarmy—and a cheater— made me wonder if he'd simply take my ideas and launch his own development campaign. I wouldn't put it past him. Especially if the other potential investors showed enough interest.

"Relax. Your muscles have tensed up on me," the woman giving me the massage whispered in my ear.

Ranger squeezed my hand. "What's wrong, beautiful?"

"Nothing. Just habit, I guess." That response made no sense, but rather than question me more, he squeezed my hand a second time.

Maybe it was the lack of rest the night before, but when I flipped to my back for the second half of my massage, I fell asleep. I hated when I did that. It felt rude. The other part of it was that I slept through *feeling* my muscles being soothed. What was the point of the massage if you didn't get to feel it?

Ranger walked the massage therapists to the door, came back, and sat beside me on the bed. "I'd say that experience did the exact opposite of what it was supposed to."

"I'm sorry." I was sulking and wished I could pull myself out of it.

"Come here." Ranger scooted up on the bed and gathered me in his arms. "I don't know about you, but I could use a nap followed by a really nice meal."

"Shouldn't it be the other way around?"

"Here's the thing. I don't want to sleep too long, so I'm counting on hunger to wake me up." He snuggled me closer. "Come on, let's sleep."

I didn't. I lay awake, worrying about the upcoming meeting. I wasn't fully prepared. That was part of my problem. I also wondered how bad it would be if I contacted my friend and asked him to uninvite Mr. Smarmy.

"You're still tense."

"I'm sorry," I repeated, wriggling out of his arms and getting up from the bed. "There's something I need to tell you."

He tucked his elbows under him and leaned up.

"I have a presentation to a potential investment group in Lake Placid on Friday."

He counted on his fingers. "That's four days from now." His eyes scrunched. "Are you worried I'll be in the way?"

"No. Yes. No."

"Glad we got that straightened out." Ranger rolled off the bed and walked over to me. "It's your meeting, beautiful. I won't interfere. I know how to make myself scarce." He chuckled. "Hiding in plain sight is kind of what I do for a living."

Hearing him say he'd be there, although not visible, made me feel better and worse at the same time. I'd never been skittish about a presentation. Why was I now? It made no sense, but I couldn't shake the feeling that something was going to go terribly wrong.

He cupped my cheek. "Talk to me."

"There's a guy who will be there…"

His eyes scrunched momentarily, the reaction vanishing so quickly I would've missed it if I hadn't been paying close attention.

"He's a jerk and…"

"Someone you were once involved with."

I nodded.

His expression softened. "No matter how much I might want to, I promise not to beat him up. Unless he touches you, of course."

While I laughed, it was forced.

"Come sit and tell me more about him. Start with his name."

"It's Maxim," I said, sitting next to him on the end of the bed. "He was in the MBA program at Tuck."

"Go on."

"We dated for a while. Until I found out he was in a long-term relationship with someone else."

"Scumbag," he muttered under his breath.

"He played it off like it was nothing, but the friend who told me about the other woman said it was pretty serious."

Ranger lay back on the bed and put his hand on my shoulder so I did the same. "Tell me what you want, Maisie. I'll do whatever it is, even if you want me to go back to Canada Lake."

"That's the last thing I want."

He let out an audible sigh. "Do you want me to be in the meeting?"

"I think so." Again, since when was I indecisive? I rubbed my chest, where I felt the dread the most.

"You don't have to decide right now, but tell me what's got you all worked up. Is it that you still have feelings for him?"

I nodded. "Feelings of disgust."

Ranger laughed and rolled to his side so he was facing me. "There's more to this."

"There is, but I can't explain it."

He stroked my hair. "Let's get some lunch. I don't know about you, but I always feel better after I've eaten."

"My grandmother would say I need a glass of sherry."

"Then, let's pick a place that serves it."

"Ranger?"

"Yeah, beautiful?"

"Thanks for not pressing me on this."

"If you figure out what is causing you so much anxiety, I'll be more than happy to listen. Otherwise, I'm just here for whatever you need."

"What a lucky girl I am."

He put his finger on my chin and turned my head so our eyes met. "I'm the lucky one."

After lunch, we walked up and down the main thoroughfare, and when the opportunity presented itself, Ranger would ask the shopkeepers if they had other locations or if they'd considered expanding into other markets. I was surprised by the number who said they'd be interested in hearing more about the development at our lake. The positive feedback left me feeling more optimistic. The dread wasn't gone entirely, but it certainly lessened.

Unfortunately, it only lasted a couple of hours. We were at dinner when my cell phone rang, and while I knew it was rude to look at it, I had to make sure it wasn't one of my grandparents calling. It wasn't. It was Maxim.

11

Ranger

When Maisie looked at her cell phone, then set it facedown on the table, I had a suspicion about who was calling. I wouldn't ask, though. If she wanted to tell me—or when she was ready—she would.

In the meantime, I'd asked Diesel to see what he could find with the little information I had. Maxim was an unusual enough name and the graduating class of Tuck's MBA program was small enough that I hoped he'd be successful without my needing to ask Maisie more about him.

"Excuse me. Ladies' room," she said, getting up and leaving the table after her phone pinged. She was clearly distraught, but in order for me to get closer to her, be a part of her life, she had to trust me. That included trusting me not to push her to talk about something she wasn't ready to.

I used the opportunity to check for an update from Diesel. There was an email, but when I clicked on it and saw its length, I decided to wait until I had a few minutes alone. If there was anything Diesel wanted me to see immediately, he would've sent it in a secure text.

"Everything okay?" I asked when Maisie returned a couple of minutes later.

"No." Her abrupt response stunned me.

"Anything you want to talk about?"

Maisie looked around the room. "Not now, but later, definitely."

Now I was anxious to read Diesel's email. We'd ordered and eaten our appetizers, but the main course had yet to be delivered. Since we were in another of our hotel's restaurants tonight, a solution was easy. "We can take our food back to the room if you'd like."

She nodded. "That would be a good idea."

"Let me see if I can track someone down."

Maisie reached out and took my hand when I stood. "Thank you, Ranger."

I leaned down and kissed her cheek. "Be right back."

I saw our waiter at the bar, made my request, and passed him a fifty when he said he'd take care of it right away.

"Let's go," I said, returning to the table and helping her with her chair.

"What's got you so spooked?" I asked once we were in the room.

"Maxim called and requested we get together before Friday's meeting. That in itself wasn't a big deal, until he said he was in Saratoga Springs *as well* and could meet either tonight or in the morning. How in the hell did he know I was here?"

"Excellent question."

"I haven't spoken to him since before we graduated. In fact, I was surprised when our mutual friend said he asked to join us."

"There's something I need to tell you. I asked one of my colleagues to see what he could find on the guy."

"And?"

"I received an email on the subject but haven't read it yet."

"Can you read it now?"

I pulled out my phone and perused it before reading the pertinent parts out loud. "Maxim Edwards, right?"

Maisie nodded.

"Seems he was being investigated for multiple counts of securities fraud. He was about to be indicted, and suddenly, the whole thing went away."

"Why?"

"Diesel, that's my colleague, believes Edwards must've made a deal. Still, court proceedings are a matter of public record. There should be something about the case being continued, dismissed, or sealed. He's digging deeper since the dollar amount of the alleged fraud is significant."

"What does that mean?"

"Apparently, he bilked investors out of close to a hundred million dollars. Maybe more."

"Why does he want to meet with me?"

"That's an excellent question. I'd like to talk it over with Diesel, if you don't mind."

"Should I alert our mutual friend? I'm sure he wouldn't want Maxim to be a part of this meeting if he was aware of the charges against him."

"Before you do that, let me check on this mutual acquaintance. In fact, can you get a list of everyone who is supposed to be at the meeting?"

Maisie picked up the hotel's notepad from the desk, swiped her phone, and wrote the list I requested.

"Thank you," I said when she handed it to me. "With your permission, I'll get this over to Diesel."

"Of course."

"I'll also alert him that Edwards is in the vicinity. If anyone has been trailing us, I have no doubt he's already picked up on it."

"Diesel is here?"

"He is."

"Am I allowed to ask the name of anyone with him?"

"Buster."

Maisie put her hand over her mouth to cover her reaction. "Seriously?"

It was such a relief—and a joy—to see her smile. "You know, we're only an hour from home. If you want to head back, we can."

"Is that what you want to do?"

I put my arms around Maisie's waist and drew her body close to mine. "I already told you I'm in no hurry to return to a place where we don't share a bed."

"Who's to say we can't share one when we're home?"

"Good point. However, my place is overrun with a bunch of guys most of the time and your grandparents…"

"It might be easier to get rid of the guys than them."

My mind immediately went to what would entail and how quickly I could make it happen. There was a knock on the door, and while I hoped it was the waiter with our dinner, I wasn't taking any chances.

"Stay over here," I said, pointing to the wall near the bed where she wouldn't be visible. I had my hand on my gun as I walked over and looked through the peephole. It was the waiter and another man I remembered seeing in the restaurant, but I still wouldn't assume that a guy who didn't think much of stealing a hundred million bucks wasn't be lurking in the shadows.

When I opened the door, I did make eye contact with a third person—Diesel. He gave a head nod, and I invited the other two to bring our food in.

"We brought dessert too, sir," said the guy I'd given the fifty to. "It's on the house."

"Thanks," I muttered, peeling off a couple more twenties.

"Would you like me to open your wine?"

"I think I can handle it." I motioned to the door.

"If you need anything else, my name is Sam."

"Got it," I said, closing it almost on his heels.

"You carry a gun," said Maisie, her eyes focused on it.

"Never leave home without it."

She walked over to the dinner trays and pulled off the first silver plate cover. "This smells so good."

She'd ordered seared duck with an amaretto-cherry sauce, and I'd gotten beef short ribs with shallots, garlic, and crushed tomato. The scents wafting from both were mouthwatering. I hoped whoever the Canada Lake Hotel hired as their chef would be able to prepare food at this level.

We sat at the table near the window, and I lit the fireplace. Regardless of the reason, I much preferred the way our evening had turned out.

"How about some music?" I took out my phone, opened an app, and selected a jazz playlist. "The speaker isn't the greatest—"

"I think everything is perfect, Ranger. The food, the company, the music—it's all so romantic."

I pulled the chair over so I could sit next to her rather than across the table. I'd known Maisie for years, but in the last few days, I found myself hoping that the way we were tonight, was the way we'd be for the rest of our lives.

After dinner, Maisie drew us a bath while I checked in with Diesel.

"Any sign this asshole is actually in town?"

"None. You're sure Maisie didn't inform anyone where she was going?"

"Her grandparents." They were the kind of people who probably wouldn't think anything of telling one of Maisie's friends that she was in Saratoga Springs.

"Makes sense. Anyway, Wasp and Swan are here now too."

"How do the big bosses at K19 feel about that?"

"Your boss, Onyx, approved it. Doesn't matter what anyone else thinks."

"Yeah, this will take some getting used to. Listen, I gotta go. Thanks for the update, Diesel."

"I'd tell you to sleep well, but that's probably the last thing you want to do."

I ended the call, shedding clothes as I went into the bathroom, where Maisie waited. She'd lit candles, poured the bottle of late-harvest wine that was delivered with our dessert, and had the same jazz playlist I had on her phone.

"I was getting lonesome and a little chilly in here all by myself."

"I think I have a few ideas about how I can warm you up."

"What did you find out?" she asked as I climbed into the bath and settled behind her.

"Not much." I told her my theory about how her grandparents had probably been the ones who let Edwards know she was here.

"Makes sense. I guess I'll have to ask them not to do that."

"We can come up with a way that doesn't make it seem like there's anything untoward going on. Maybe phrase it in such a way that since you and I are dating…"

"Is that what we're doing?"

"Along with sleeping together, but you phrase it however you want."

Maisie laughed. "Your way is probably better."

I moved her hair from her neck like I had the last time we were in the tub and scattered kisses on her shoulder.

"You think we should go back to the lake, don't you?"

"I do. At least until we can get a better idea of what this guy is up to."

"I agree." Her voice sounded as disappointed as I felt.

12

Maisie

We'd only spent two—wonderful and amazing—nights here, and we were already going home. The disappointment I felt was profound on two levels. First, I loved being with Ranger. It didn't matter what we were doing. Second, I was serious about the research I needed to do in order to be prepared for my meeting on Friday. If it took place.

I was able to assemble some data from what I'd gotten from the chamber of commerce, but most of what I needed was potential-based, which meant I'd need numbers that were nearly impossible to get.

As if preparing for the meeting wasn't stressful enough, now I had to deal with fucking Maxim Edwards and wonder what the hell he wanted after all this time.

Actually, that wasn't difficult to figure out. If he was in legal trouble, if what Ranger said was true about him being indicted—regardless of whether the charges had mysteriously disappeared—he'd be looking for money. My projects wouldn't net him a hundred million dollars, but if he was able to dupe other people out of that much, who was to say he couldn't get a few million out of me in order to tide him over.

God, I rued the day I met the *sonuvabitch.* I'd been taken in by his handsome face and charming manner. Ranger had more substance than that, right? I prayed so. Wait. *I knew so.* The two men were nothing alike. Well, apart from being handsome and charming.

And right now, quiet.

"Is everything okay?" I asked when we were within a few minutes of our camps.

"Honestly? No."

I turned in my seat. "What's wrong?"

I saw him flex his hands. First his right, then his left. I'd noticed him do it a couple of times before.

"You're going to think I'm nuts."

"Doubtful."

"I'm crazy about you, Maisie."

"The feeling is mutual."

He looked out the side window, then back at me. "It might be a little more for me."

"Me too."

I almost laughed when he rolled his shoulders, but he seemed so bothered I didn't want to make light of the way he was feeling.

"You know, I've always hated the kind of movies where a couple falls in love in five minutes and they live happily ever after."

"Me too," I repeated. "Except with me, it's more books I read."

"I mean, it isn't like we haven't known each other. We have. For years. Although we didn't really date then. I would've. You know, if the timing had been better."

I put my hand on his arm. "Ranger, is there a point to this?"

"Back to the crazy-train part."

"Come on, whatever it is, just say it."

"I don't want to take you to your grandparents' camp. I don't want to sleep without you in my bed tonight. In fact, I don't ever want to spend another night apart. I know that's impossible, given what I do for a living, but if I have the choice, I want to spend every night I can with you. And not just nights. Days. Every day. Every night. How nuts is that?"

Like he had, I rolled my shoulders and took a deep breath. "You probably aren't going to believe me when I say I feel the same way."

He turned to me, eyes scrunched. "You do?"

"Especially the crazy-train part. I mean, for me. When I think about us, I feel like I'm rushing things and you're going to run for the hills."

"We agreed not to overthink how we were feeling."

I laughed. "I never dreamed you could possibly be feeling the same way I am."

"Your grandparents think we're going to be gone a few more days."

"Our camps aren't that far apart. They'll *see* us."

Ranger nodded. "Why did I think coming back was a good idea?"

"We aren't there yet. Maybe just leaving Saratoga Springs was enough?"

"Are you asking?"

"What about our 'company'?"

He chuckled. "They've been bored out of their minds. This is the most excitement they've had in a couple of weeks. I could make it really interesting by turning the car around and not telling them what we're doing."

"Will you get in trouble?"

"As Diesel keeps reminding me, I'm second-in-command."

"Who's first?"

"Onyx, and he'll love that we're being so spontaneous." Ranger pulled over. "Should we resume our trip and head to Lake George?"

"Actually, there's a place on Long Lake called the Love Lodge." I rolled my eyes. "Hokey, I know, but it's one of the most popular wedding venues in the park."

Ranger's eyebrows wiggled, and I giggled.

"Not for us. I mean, you and me. But after our conversation that first night, I agree it's something the Canada Lake Hotel has to offer. Since we're located almost three hours south, it'll be easier for people throughout the state to travel to us."

"From the research I've done, weddings pull in a significant amount of income."

My eyes scrunched. "Research?"

He looked over at me with a sheepish grin. "I've been doing some."

"On wedding venues?"

His cheeks actually turned pink. "Among other things."

My heart warmed. It seemed as though Ranger was as into this economic redevelopment project as I was. Maybe it was because he was bored, but I was enjoying it so much more, having someone as enthusiastic as him to bounce ideas off. "Thank you."

"You're welcome. Um, what for?"

"Everything. Being so…wonderful."

He brought my hand to his lips and kissed my palm. "Okay, copilot. Let's hurry up and get to the *Love Lodge*."

I bit my lower lip. "I hope I can get a reservation."

"Tuesday in January. I think we'll be okay. It's been years since I've been to the area. What else should we see while we're there?"

While Ranger drove, I made a two-night reservation at the lodge along with dinner reservations for tonight, massage reservations for tomorrow—as a surprise to him this time—and a list of other things we should do and see while we were there.

I rested against the seat and closed my eyes. I'd never been happier at any other time in my life. The crap with Maxim was a blight, but one I could easily overlook. I promised myself that if he was at the meeting on Friday, I wouldn't let him derail me. Especially with Ranger by my side.

When we pulled up, the first thing I noticed was the huge barn that sat as close to the lake as the lodge did. I hadn't seen anything on their website about that. I pulled out my notepad and sketched out the Canada Lake Hotel's footprint along with the amount of open space surrounding it. While there wouldn't be room for something as large as this barn, we could definitely fit something half its size.

"Look," said Ranger, pointing to a small chapel adjacent to it.

"They've got big, small, and everything in between covered."

"It looks like it's been here longer than the lodge. Let's go check it out."

Ranger pulled up on the far side of the parking lot, and we got out.

"Hello there! Welcome to Love Chapel," said a man coming out the front door. He looked like Santa Claus wearing a minister's collar.

Ranger and I introduced ourselves, and I explained where we were from and why we were there.

He raised a brow and winked. "Are you sure that's the only reason you're here?"

I shuffled my feet and rubbed my arms. It was cold right off the big lake. "Um, may we go inside?"

"By all means," he said. "We'll see you two later at the lodge. Enjoy!"

When Ranger opened the door and I walked inside, a feeling I couldn't explain swept over me. I was curious on so many levels. How long had this chapel been here? Who had built it? Were the wooden pews, walls, and altar rails all hand carved like they looked? And most importantly, why did being here feel like coming home? I'd never been in a chapel like this one, yet I'd never felt so welcome or so at peace.

"Do you mind if we sit for a minute?" I asked Ranger.

"I was about to say the same thing."

I sat in the third row from the front on the left side and looked at the painting above the altar. It was of Jesus' ascension.

"I know it sounds crazy, but I feel like I've been here before," said Ranger. "Only one of many crazy things I seem to be saying and doing today."

"Maybe you have been."

He shook his head. "I don't remember anything else about this place. Not the lake nor the lodge or even the grounds."

Odd that we both felt the same way. We sat in the chapel for quite a while, neither of us speaking. I didn't feel the need to, and neither did Ranger.

"Ready to keep exploring?" he asked at the same time I was about to say something similar.

"I am."

He held my hand as we walked outside and over to the lodge to check in. The same man who met us outside the chapel was behind the front desk in the lobby.

"Welcome to Love Lodge," he said. "Did you enjoy visiting the chapel?"

"We both felt like we've been here before, but neither of us remembers it."

He nodded. "I've heard this a time or two."

I looked to the left and saw a closed door. Above it, a sign read, Long Lake Town Clerk. "What is that?" I asked.

"After the Great Fire of 1910, the lodge and chapel were the only buildings left standing on the property and in much of the town." He motioned toward the door. "The clerk, the only town official then and now, moved in here. Never saw a reason to move out, I guess."

"The website says you host a lot of weddings."

There was a twinkle in the man's eyes. "Some planned, some unplanned."

"What does that mean?" Ranger asked.

"Town clerk right here on the premises. Plus, the magistrate lives next door. You'd be surprised how many elopements we host."

I thought about it for a minute. "So people come and get their marriage license here at the town clerk's office. Then the judge waives the waiting period?"

"You're catching on."

"Brilliant," I said under my breath. It was the kind of thing we could do at the Canada Lake Hotel too since the town clerk and court were located virtually across the road.

"One room?"

"That's right." I was really far from a prude, but I felt my face flush when the *minister* asked the question.

"Will you be joining us for dinner tonight?"

I looked at Ranger, who nodded. "Yes," he answered when I nodded in return. "Do you have a table available at seven?"

The man raised his eyebrow. "Six would be better."

"Six it is." Ranger winked at me, and we both stifled a chuckle.

"Do you need assistance with your bags?"

"I've got it, but thanks."

I wondered about our "company," but since I hadn't had anything to do with them checking into the other hotel, I didn't worry about this one.

"Would it be possible for me to take a look at the wedding reception venues?" I asked.

"By all means," he responded like he had when I'd asked about entering the chapel. "The barn is open, and if you want to see the main dining hall before dinner, just go through the door at the end of the hall. Would you like a brochure as well?"

"Please." He went in a door behind the front desk. I was beginning to wonder if Pastor Santa ran this place all by himself. Surely, there must be more staff somewhere.

"Do you feel like we're in the twilight zone?" Ranger asked.

"Totally."

He came back out and handed me an envelope. "I let Mabel know you're heading her way. She has the afternoon wine and cheese reception all set up too."

"How nice. Thank you." I waved over my shoulder when Ranger and I went in the direction of the dining room.

13

Ranger

"A glass of wine sounds perfect right now."

I had to agree. What I'd said a couple of minutes ago about feeling like I was in an alternate dimension grew more intense with every passing minute. It wasn't unpleasant, just odd. And disconcerting. Mainly because it was as though Maisie and I were supposed to be here. Was that why I'd been compelled to turn the car around earlier and not return to either of our camps first? If we had, would we have changed our mind about heading out again, or would we have just stayed at our own cabin?

There was more to it than even that, none of which I could say out loud, especially to Maisie.

"What? Is it bad?" she asked when I made a face after taking a sip of wine.

"No. It's good."

She giggled. "Looks like it. I can't wait to try it myself."

I took another drink, this time more of a gulp. "Really, it's very good."

She took a tentative sip. "It is. So, why the weird face?"

"This place is…"

Maisie nodded. "I get it. Weird isn't the right word. I mean, it's wonderful, just…"

"Unusual."

"We can go with that," she said, laughing.

"Oh, hello!" a woman said, coming out of the kitchen with a platter of appetizers. "You must be Own and Maisie."

"Owen."

She looked down at a piece of paper. "Sorry, Dipper's handwriting is atrocious."

"Did you say Dipper?" Maisie burst out laughing.

"Our grandkids started calling him that. I'm Grammy Mabel, and he's Grampy Dipper."

"I don't get it," I whispered.

"It's from a cartoon."

Just add one more bizarre thing to the Love Lodge list.

"Have the two of you been here before? You look so familiar."

"We were commenting earlier that we felt like we had, but no."

"Come, dear. Have a plate. These are the most popular wedding menu items."

Mabel handed an overflowing plate to Maisie.

"We can share," I said when I saw her putting together a second one.

"Suit yourself. There's a nice table by the window that looks out over the lake."

"I feel like I'm in one of those Christmas movies but three weeks after," Maisie whispered when we sat at the table Mabel pointed out to us. "Oh my God, try this one," she said, handing me something wrapped in dough.

"Wow." I grabbed a couple more and popped them in my mouth.

"Do you think the story he told about people eloping here is true?"

I looked over my shoulder and saw Mabel walking in our direction, carrying the bottle of wine. "Hang on and I'll answer."

"Which are your favorites?" she asked, refilling both of our glasses.

I pointed to the one remaining dough-wrapped brie with cranberry sauce.

"I'll bring more of those," Mabel offered.

Maisie held up one finger, then pointed to her mouth. Mabel waited. "If you bring more, we won't eat any dinner."

"Don't be silly. Of course you'll still eat dinner. Just like all your wedding guests will."

"Does she know something we don't?" Maisie joked when Mabel went back into the kitchen. "Ranger?" she said when I didn't respond. "Is everything okay?"

Maybe it was the wine or just being at this crazy place, but I found myself wishing Maisie and I *were* getting married. I scooted our chairs closer, and she looked at me with wide eyes.

"Would it be that crazy?"

She took another sip of wine and set her glass on the table. "What?"

"You and me. Getting married."

"You're serious."

While she hadn't phrased it as a question, I nodded anyway.

She took a deep breath and let it out slowly. "When?"

I leaned forward and stared into her eyes but didn't say anything.

"Ranger?"

I put my arm around her. "Don't you feel it, Maisie? Am I wrong?"

"About what?" she said so softly I could barely hear her.

"Us. From that very first day on the dock to your eighteenth birthday party to the night I walked into your grandparents' camp and told you it had been my intention to claim you. I still feel the same way. You're mine, Maisie. You always have been."

"Are you suggesting we get married here? Now?"

I shook my head. "I'm asking. If you want me to, I'll get down on one knee."

"Wait," she said when I pushed my chair back as if I was going to.

"I'm crazy, right? That's what you're going to say?"

She slowly shook her head. "Not even close."

"What, then?"

"I feel it too."

"I knew you did. Maisie, I love—"

"Don't say it yet."

"Why not?"

"Wait until tonight."

I smiled. "Yeah?"

"Yeah."

"Should we go find Dipper?" As soon as I said his name, he walked into the dining room.

"What can I help you two with?"

"Is the town clerk around?"

Dipper smiled. "Let me go get her from the kitchen."

"And the judge?"

"He can be here in a jiffy."

"What do we need?" Maisie asked.

"Just your identification. We can add the other items to your file later." He winked.

"Are you really a minister?"

"Fully ordained thirty years now, Miss Jones."

She turned to me. "Are we really doing this?"

"Only if you want to."

"But you do?"

"More than anything else in the world."

"Better go get the clerk and the judge, then," she said to Dipper.

I so wanted to say the words she wouldn't let me a couple of minutes ago. Tonight, she wouldn't be able to stop me.

"Um, what about our company? I'd rather they not know before my grandparents."

"I'm with you on that, and I'll handle it."

"I hear there's some paperwork you two would like to fill out," said Mabel, who had taken off the apron she was wearing earlier. "Come with me."

We followed her to the lobby and waited while she unlocked the door with the town clerk sign above it. It took us less than five minutes to complete the documents that would change our lives forever.

"Come with me," Mabel repeated, but this time she was speaking only to Maisie. She patted my cheek before they walked away. "You'll see her in a little over an hour."

"Where are they going?" I asked Dipper.

"To get ready."

"Oh, crap. I haven't brought our bags in yet."

"Maisie won't really need it, but I'll take it to her anyway. You know, in case she wants to put on a little makeup."

"I brought a sports coat, dress shirt, and a pair of slacks. No tie, though."

"You'd be surprised how often I hear that."

I led him out to my SUV, and while he took Maisie's bag to her, I called Diesel.

"What the fuck are you up to?" he said, skipping any kind of greeting.

"We changed our mind."

"Clearly. Didn't think it was important to respond to any of my texts?"

"Sorry. Is there anything I need to know?" I silently prayed there wasn't. Now that Maisie and I had set this plan in motion, I didn't want anything to interfere with it.

"Only me looking for answers. I finally called Onyx."

"Listen. I need a favor."

"What's that?"

I had no idea how to ask while not giving anything away. "I need some privacy tonight. Between six and seven."

"How close can we be?"

"We won't be leaving the property."

"I see."

"I'd rather you didn't."

"You know how to reach me in the event of an emergency."

"I do."

"The crew and I are staying at the place next door. We'll stand down until you signal us. One way or another."

"I appreciate this."

"I hope whatever it is, is important."

It was the most important thing I'd done in my life.

14

Maisie

"Thanks," I said when Dipper dropped my bag off in our room. Somehow, I doubted Ranger had booked the honeymoon suite earlier, but that's where Mabel said we'd be spending the night.

"What is his real name?" I asked when he closed the door behind him.

"Charlie MacIntosh, but everyone's been calling him Dipper for the last couple of years. He likes it." She walked over to a closet I hadn't noticed near the door. "There's something I want you to see."

When she pulled it out, I gasped.

"Whose is that?"

"It was mine. Hard to believe I used to be the same size you are now. Would you like to try it on?"

A part of me felt like it was too much, but wasn't it all too much? Wasn't this as surreal as everything else that had happened between Ranger and me, not just in the last few days, but since the day we first met? He'd admitted he had feelings for me in the same way I did for him.

"I would love to."

Mabel placed the most beautiful wrap around my shoulders and led me through the lodge. "Don't worry. You're our only guests tonight, and Dipper and Owen are already at the chapel. Judge Thomas and his wife, Cora, are there too. They can serve as your witnesses. Oh, and Cora plays the piano."

"You've thought of everything."

"Why do you think they call this the Love Lodge, sweetheart?"

"I just thought that was the name."

"Goodness, no. Back when it was built, it was known as Long Lake Lodge. Not quite as romantic, right?"

We were about to step out a side door when panic overcame me. "My grandparents. They'll be so hurt I didn't tell them."

Mabel shook her head. "Al and Mary will understand better than most."

I was stunned. "Do you know them?"

"I was a few years younger than they were, so I wasn't allowed to watch, but where do you think they got married?"

"You aren't serious."

"I am."

That explained why this place seemed so familiar. The photos I'd seen were all in black and white and not taken by a professional photographer. That's why I hadn't recognized the chapel. Along with the fact that the trees on the property had grown so much taller in the years in between.

"You really don't think they'll be upset?"

"I doubt they told their parents—or their grandparents." Mabel put her hands on my shoulders. "Ready to go marry the love of your life?"

"He is, you know."

"Of course I do, dear. Otherwise, we wouldn't have the judge sign off on the waiting period."

The chapel looked even more beautiful. Maybe it was because the lighting was more dramatic since it was dark outside. The same familiar feeling as earlier in the day came over me. And a sense of peace. The worry I had over my grandparents being hurt or angry faded away when I raised my head and saw the look on Ranger's face.

Cora began to play, and I walked toward him. It didn't matter that there was no one by my side. As soon as I reached the front of the chapel, he would be. Not just for now, but in my heart, I knew we'd be together forever.

My eyes filled with tears when I saw his were, but we were both smiling too.

"Dearly beloved," Dipper began. I heard little of what he said as I stared into my love's eyes.

When it came to our vows, Ranger interrupted him. "We each have something we want to say at the end."

Dipper smiled and we continued.

"I, Owen Messick, take thee, Maisie Ann Jones, to be my wedded wife, to have and to hold from this day forward, for better, for worse, for richer, for poorer, in sickness and in health, to love and to cherish, till death do us part, according to God's holy ordinance; and thereto I pledge thee my faith."

I repeated the words back to him, then looked at Dipper, who nodded.

"I love you, Owen."

"I love you, Maisie."

15

Ranger

Never in my life had I seen a vision more beautiful, more breathtaking than Maisie when she walked in the door of the chapel. Mabel helped remove a wrap from around her shoulders, and I gasped. The pale cream-colored lace dress she wore looked as though it had been made for her.

She slowly walked toward me, and my eyes filled with tears of joy. No decision I'd made in my life was better than this one. We were meant to spend our lives together.

Waiting until the end of our vows to profess our love felt right too, especially since the next thing we heard was Dipper saying we were husband and wife.

The kiss we shared was harder, deeper, more passionate than any that had come before it. I saw it as a promise of the love we'd share, not just between her and me, but with the family I hoped we'd be blessed with. Maybe it was something we should've discussed before we took this giant leap, but it was only one of many things we hadn't. We'd figure out whatever came our way together, making decisions together.

Maisie put her palm on my cheek. "You're deep in thought."

I shrugged. "I was just thinking that whatever life brings us, we'll figure out together."

"I like the sound of that very much."

"Who's ready for dinner?" asked Mabel. "We can serve you in the dining room or in the honeymoon suite. Whichever you prefer."

"Honeymoon suite?" I mouthed.

Maisie nodded. "I think Dipper and Mabel moved us." She stepped closer and put her mouth near my ear. "I'd rather have dinner there."

I had to agree. Preferably with far fewer clothes on.

"By the way, where did you find this dress?" I asked when we were changing before our dinner was delivered and Maisie asked me to help with her zipper.

"I think it came with the room. Although Mabel did say she wore it for her wedding. Oh, and I haven't told you, but this is where my grandparents got married."

"You're kidding?"

She shook her head. "Mabel knows them."

This place and its history got more surreal with every passing minute. What were the odds we'd end up at the same place Al and Mary were married only to decide to elope like they had?

We spent two nights at the Love Lodge, and while I'd asked Maisie if she wanted to postpone her meeting in Lake Placid, she said that as long as I didn't mind, she'd rather get it over with.

Diesel hadn't found a connection between the other people on Maisie's list of attendees and Maxim Edwards, who as far as I knew, still planned to be there. I'd be by her side, so his presence didn't worry me.

We also discussed inviting Diesel as well as Swan, who would pose as a couple interested in investing in Canada Lake's redevelopment. Wasp and Buster would remain behind the scenes, both with orders to pay close attention to Edwards in particular.

Since we spent the last two nights doing nothing but enjoying our honeymoon, Maisie was frazzled and feeling unprepared.

"This is a preliminary meeting, beautiful. You have the initial information packets ready. You are an expert on not just Canada Lake but the surrounding area. I've done enough of my own research that I can chime in if necessary as well."

Her eyes opened wide. "Who will we say you are?"

"Your business partner."

She studied me. "Are you?"

"I would like to be your partner in all things, but that's your decision. For tomorrow's meeting, we can certainly play it off that way. Just know that I believe in you and your ideas. If asked, I can honestly answer that I made the decision to invest after our first conversation."

"You did?"

"Absolutely."

She launched herself into my arms and kissed me. It was something I planned to enjoy as often as possible for the rest of my life.

"Is everything okay with you?" Diesel asked later when we were in the living room of the suite we'd reserved and I'd finished briefing the team on their roles.

"Never better. Why?"

"That's what I mean. Look, I know getting laid puts everyone into a better mood, but you're over the top."

I hated him using that particular expression when talking about my *wife*, but Maisie and I had agreed that until we told her grandparents and my parents, we didn't want anyone else to know we were married.

"Yep, that's what it is. Are we all set?"

He raised a brow but shrugged it off and left the room like the others had. Maisie came out of the suite's bedroom.

"Is everyone ready for tomorrow?" she asked.

"This is tame by our typical mission standards." I realized that probably wasn't the right thing to say when she put a hand on her hip. "But no less important," I added.

When I sat on the sofa, Maisie sat beside me. "It's nice to be alone again. Although I'm a little sad to be missing the band at Sherman's this weekend, especially since I invited Onyx and your brother to go with us."

"I'd forgotten all about that, and no offense to you, but I'm sure they did too." Between Jimmy's separation and Onyx not being able to be with the woman he loved—because of the threat against K19—I doubted either man wanted to go to a place where there'd be other couples dancing.

"Maybe next weekend."

I nodded, but I had other plans. Since everyone believed we were traveling to research the areas of the park that drew the most tourists, there was no reason we needed to hurry back. Once the meeting was over tomorrow and we determined Edwards' reason for wanting to be in attendance, there was a good chance we'd be able to send two of the people traveling with us home. I'd let Diesel decide which two, unless Onyx had an opinion, of course.

Maisie stood, and I expected her to walk away. Instead, she moved my arms and sat on my lap.

"Mmm." I nuzzled her neck. "I like this."

"Since, according to you, I am prepared for tomorrow, I thought we could get back to honeymooning."

I stood with her in my arms and carried her into the bedroom.

"I never dreamed I could be this happy," she said when I set her on the bed and undressed her.

"I feel the same way." I said the words, but in the back of my mind, I had an immediate and powerful premonition. *Impending doom.*

"Are you sure?" Maisie asked, studying me.

"I'll feel better once we're done with Edwards."

She nodded. "You and me both."

By the next morning, the bad feeling had gotten significantly worse, and I said as much to Diesel when he and Swan arrived.

"Maybe we should rethink having Buster and Wasp on the outside."

"I agree."

There were six unknowns attending this meeting and five of us, counting Maisie. Even without counting her, we outnumbered them on experience and firepower alone.

"Have two more copies of the prospectus made and advise the guys to dress the part."

"Roger that. Anything else, boss?"

I looked up at Diesel, expecting to see a smirk. I didn't. As he'd reminded me before, I *was* his boss, and it was time I acted like it. "Not at this time."

16

Maisie

I was a nervous wreck, and while he tried to hide it, I could tell Ranger was anxious too.

Fifteen minutes before I expected anyone to arrive, there was a knock at the door. I dropped the water I'd been holding.

"I've got it," said Swan, rushing over to clean up the broken glass on the tile floor.

"Ready?" Ranger asked.

"No. Yes. No."

He leaned close to me. "Glad we cleared that up," he whispered, making me smile. "Let's do this."

As I feared, Maxim stood at the door when I opened it. He'd arrived early and alone. When he stepped forward as though he intended to embrace me, I took two steps back. "I was surprised when William called and said you wanted to join us today."

"Hello, Maisie. It's good to see you too."

"I didn't say it was good to see you, Maxim."

His eyes scrunched, and he lowered his voice. "Is this how you intend to play this?"

"Play this?" I seethed. "If this is some kind of game to you, I'll go ahead and ask you to leave now."

I could feel Ranger approach behind me. "Hello, I'm Owen Messick, Miss Jones' partner." Ranger held out his hand, but Maxim didn't.

"No need to stand on formality. Maisie and I know each other *quite* well."

I wanted to throat punch the smarmy bastard, but probably not as much as Ranger, who stepped between us, did. "I missed your name."

"Maxim Edwards." This time, when Maxim held out his hand, Ranger ignored it.

"You're a guest of?"

"William Schilling."

"I see. Given Mr. Schilling has yet to arrive, you can wait here."

Ranger didn't invite Maxim to take a seat or come farther into the room, so I didn't either.

"I'm sorry," I whispered when we were on the other side of the suite and around the corner.

"Absolutely nothing for you to be sorry for. It's all on him. Like a stench, in fact."

I put my hand over my mouth to stifle a giggle. Ranger pulled it away and kissed me instead. "I love you, Maisie."

"I love you too." I raised my head and saw Maxim standing almost directly behind Ranger.

"Partners, is it?"

"What it is, is none of your business," I spat under my breath. "I think you should leave."

There was another knock at the door, and I brushed past him. I knew he and Ranger had words, but I couldn't hear them.

"Is Maxim here already?" asked William when I offered to take his coat, something I hadn't done for the other man.

"Yes, but I believe he's leaving."

"Maisie, is this William?" Ranger asked, walking up next to me. "Owen Messick. Pleasure to meet you."

The two men shook. I'd always liked William and was relieved when, a couple of days ago, Ranger had said there was no evidence he was mixed up with Maxim's securities fraud.

"What's this about you leaving?" William asked.

"Misunderstanding." Maxim looked at his watch. "I thought I had a conflict, but it's been resolved."

I wouldn't look at Ranger now, but obviously, he had a reason for wanting the asshole to stay.

The four others we were expecting arrived, and we gathered around the suite's large table, where Ranger's colleagues were already seated. Ranger introduced everyone and explained the other people in attendance were brought in as potential investors as well.

Maxim cleared his throat. "I hope you have room for a few more."

"You're this anxious already without even seeing the prospectus?" William laughed. Maxim glared at me, and I glared back. Maybe Ranger expected me to handle this more professionally, but I couldn't. Seeing his arrogant mug made me hate the cheater all the more.

"Shall we get started?" Ranger asked. I took it from there.

Maxim interrupted several times with questions I would eventually answer, and Ranger asked if he would be *kind* enough to wait until the end of the presentation. I almost laughed, but continued.

When I reached the last page of the prospectus, Diesel and Buster both started talking before Maxim could, asking many of the same questions he had but worded differently.

Finally, Maxim stood and spoke over the rest. "Maisie, you are what? Twenty-six? While you graduated from Tuck like many of the rest of us, I question your experience level. Why should anyone invest the kind of money you're asking for?"

I'd anticipated a similar question, but not worded quite the same way. Rather than letting it unnerve me, I leaned forward and rested my palms on the table.

"The answer to your question lies in the document you barely skimmed. Instead, you attempted to disrupt my presentation. Please take your time reviewing the information provided. Once you have, either my partner or I will respond to appropriate questions."

I looked around the table at the five other men I'd gone to grad school with. There wasn't a single one who didn't return my gaze with pride.

"Look, Maxim," said William, rubbing the man's shoulder. "We're all friends here, or we once were. Let's knock off the stilted formality and get down to it. If you're not prepared to negotiate, you can set up a meeting at a later date." William looked at the others. "I'm ready to move forward. How about all of you?"

I'd really hoped Maxim would get up and leave, but he didn't. He studied me while Ranger studied him. He wasn't the only one. Diesel never took his eyes off the man.

"I want someone on him around the clock," Ranger said after everyone who came for the meeting left, including Maxim.

"You got it, boss," said Buster, typing something into his phone.

"I'm sorry, Maisie. There's something about him that doesn't sit right. Couple that with the charges that vanished into thin air, and my intuition is screaming at me that there's a lot more to this than what we've been able to find out."

"I feel the same way you do." And if I weren't surrounded by people—including my *husband*—who I knew would do everything possible to keep me safe, I would be as unsettled as Ranger. Maybe even frightened.

William and the four other men in attendance had asked me to send investment agreements to them as soon as I was able. Each had offered a stepped or tiered offer of money. The amounts were more than I'd hoped for.

Unfortunately, rather than feeling relieved that I'd come face-to-face with Maxim and it was behind me, I felt more unsettled.

"I'm in no hurry to get back to the lake," Ranger said after Diesel led the others out of our suite and he and I were finally alone.

"I'm not, either." Yes, my grandparents had eloped too, but they'd been together longer than the week we had been. In my heart, I knew getting married was the right thing for us, but my brain wasn't one hundred percent on board.

Whenever I thought about telling anyone what we'd done, I worried about their reaction. Each time I "acted it out" inside my head, whoever was on the other side of the conversation appeared aghast rather than happy for us. The longer we spent away from home, the longer we could just enjoy our honeymoon without anyone casting shade on our marriage.

We decided to spend several more days in Lake Placid, given its close proximity to other big tourist draws.

17

Ranger

It had been two weeks since Maisie's meeting with investors and when we got married. Three weeks since our first date. It felt so much longer than that. Maisie and I were compatible in a way I'd never been with another person. We certainly didn't agree on everything, but we were both willing to compromise.

It was something I remembered my father had said to Jimmy the night before he got married. "Pick your battles, son. Always be willing to compromise, and you will have a happy marriage."

I knew there was a lot more to it. While I hadn't seen my mother and father argue very often, there had been times I could tell they were mad at each other.

We hadn't had our first argument yet, but we also weren't tiptoeing around each other. Maisie made me smile, warmed my heart, and kept me on the edge of desire all day, every day. Night too.

We'd gone downhill skiing at the local ski area and Nordic skiing on Lake Placid's cross-country trails, plus lots of tobogganing. She was naturally athletic like I was and always up for an adventure.

We spent three more days in the northern part of the park before heading to another lake farther south, where we spent two days.

We'd agreed to stay two more nights in Lake George, then spend the final two nights of our honeymoon in Saratoga Springs, which I considered to be the place where our relationship officially began.

Instead, I received a message earlier from Onyx, asking me to return to Canada Lake as soon as possible. Doc and Merrigan from our parent company—as he'd started referring to K19 Security Solutions—were on their way and had requested a team meeting.

"It's okay," Maisie said when I apologized. "We've been gone longer than we anticipated."

"And we got married." I winked and pulled her into my arms. "Ready to tell the world?"

When she bit her bottom lip, I had my answer.

"We don't have to just because we're going back to the lake. We can wait as long as you'd like."

"It won't bother you?"

I walked over to the end of the bed and pulled her onto my lap. "Our marriage is between you and me. While our extended families are important to me, you and I are now the nucleus of our own family."

"I like that."

"I like you." I nuzzled her neck. "Actually, I love you." Now that I'd started saying it, I wondered if maybe I did too often.

"Can I stay with you?"

I'd already given the logistics of where we'd live some thought. "Stay with me? No. Live together? Yes. We just have to talk about Jimmy. Would you be comfortable if he stayed there until he figured his life out?"

"I was going to ask if he'd be comfortable with me there."

I shook my head. "You're my wife, Maisie. I know I keep bringing it up, but it's the truth. You and I are going to be living in the camp on Canada Lake; Jimmy is staying there."

Before she could respond, my phone chimed with a call from Diesel. Since he hadn't messaged first, I knew it was a call I needed to take. "Sorry, I have to get this."

Maisie nodded, got off my lap, and went into the bathroom.

"Hey, man."

"Ranger, I've got some news. Maxim Edwards was found dead in his apartment this morning. Buster was on stakeout and was there when NYPD arrived on the scene. Evidently, one of the neighbors heard a gunshot."

"Self-inflicted?"

"I don't know yet. We're waiting for the preliminary report."

"Keep me posted. You got the message about us heading back today, right?"

"Yes, sir. We'll be ready at eleven hundred hours."

I shook my head at my best friend's formality. "Copy that."

I knocked on the bathroom door to let Maisie know I was finished with my call.

"Is everything okay?" she asked.

"Let's sit."

"Just tell me."

"Apparently, Maxim was found dead this morning. We don't have any details yet."

Maisie put her hand in front of her mouth. "Oh my God. I didn't wish for *this*."

"Of course you didn't."

"I didn't think very highly of him, though."

"My opinion was worse."

Maisie walked over and looked out the window, shaking her head. "I can't believe he's dead."

I wasn't sure what to make of her reaction, which meant I wasn't sure what to say.

"When do we need to leave?"

I looked at my watch. "About an hour."

"I know the timing is really terrible, but I need to feel close to you, Ranger."

I led her into the bedroom and held her in my arms. I could feel the dampness from her tears on my shirt and stroked her back until it was time to go.

When we arrived at the lake, Jimmy and Onyx were sitting on the front porch of the camp next door to ours. I'd already taken Maisie's and my bags upstairs, and she was unpacking her stuff.

"Got a minute?" I said to my brother.

"Of course."

When I led him into the boathouse, he turned on the radio.

"What's up?"

"Maisie is going to be moving in here."

"That's great news, bro. I'm happy for you both."

"Thanks."

Jimmy's expression changed, maybe realizing why I was talking to him on our own. "Do you want me to move out?"

"No. Absolutely not. I just wanted you to know."

"I can look for a place."

"That isn't necessary right now."

"So, are the two of you serious?"

I had to respect Maisie's feelings about not telling anyone we'd gotten married yet, and that included my brother. "Yeah, we're serious."

Another car was parked in the driveway, but closer to Blanca's camp, when we came out of the boathouse. I looked over and saw her and Onyx out on the porch, sitting on the low country swing he and my brother had built for her.

"Looks like I need to make myself scarce from there too."

I rubbed his shoulder. "You're always welcome at the camp."

"I really thought things would eventually work out between Melanie and me, but it doesn't look like that's going to happen."

"I'm sorry, Jimmy."

He walked down to the dock and looked out over the lake. I figured he needed time on his own, so I went inside.

"How did it go?" Maisie asked. "I can always go—"

I crowded her into a corner. "Wherever you go, I go too. For the rest of our lives, beautiful."

We had a quiet evening on our own. I had no idea where Jimmy went, but I knew it wasn't next door since Blanca was there. That he'd left made me feel like shit, but he was a grown man capable of making his own decisions. Who knew, maybe he went out and got lucky?

"Doc and Merrigan should be here soon, and our meeting will start shortly thereafter," I said the next morning. We'd already discussed Maisie hanging out next door with Blanca and my brother, if he made it back. "There he is," I said under my breath when he pulled in seconds later.

"Should I leave now?"

"You don't have to until they get here." I led her over to the sofa and pulled her onto my lap when I sat. "How are you feeling about being back here?"

"Okay. I mean, I'm feeling guilty about not telling my grandparents we're *married*," she whispered the last word. "But maybe after your meeting, we can tell them together."

"Sounds good to me." I didn't want to bring up the next subject, but I had to. "How are you feeling about Maxim's death?"

She rested her head on my shoulder. "I suppose I should be upset, but I'm not. I don't think he deserved to die, but he wasn't a very nice person."

"All logical feelings."

"Looks like your guests were right behind me," said Jimmy, coming in the back door.

Maisie scooted off my lap. "I'll see you later."

"I'll walk next door with you."

"How is Blanca?" I heard Merrigan ask when I returned from the other camp. I couldn't hear Onyx's response, but I did hear the next thing he said. "We're getting married."

Merrigan embraced him. "I'm so happy for you both."

I couldn't wait to tell everyone that Maisie and I were already married. My chest swelled with pride at the thought. God, I loved her.

"There you are," Merrigan said, turning to me. "Sorry you had to cut your trip short."

"It was time for us to come back anyway." We cheek kissed.

"We should get started. There's a lot we need to cover this afternoon."

I took a seat when Doc asked everyone to. He walked over and sat in the chair beside Onyx while Merrigan remained standing.

"This will be the one and only meeting I facilitate on behalf of our new unit, K19 Shadow Operations," she began. "After today, the team, along with its assignments, will be in the hands of Onyx and Ranger." Those in the room applauded.

"By now, you should've all received the final report on our last mission. If there are any questions, I'll address them. However, I'd prefer not to spend more time than is necessary on it. Because of the kill contracts United Russia put out on the partners of K19 Security Solutions, they will be forced to endure near-debilitating sanctions. We have also called for the resignation and imprisonment of their leader in order for the retributions to be lifted."

Before I could ask why we were meeting if we weren't spending any time discussing the outcome of that mission, Doc stood and handed an envelope to each person in the room other than Merrigan.

"What's this?" Onyx asked.

"Your first official mission," he answered.

Like everyone else, including Doc, I opened the envelope and scanned the first few lines.

"What is this?" Onyx repeated.

I was glad he had. I couldn't understand why we would be hired to conduct the investigation of a kidnapping and murder that would normally fall under the jurisdiction of local law enforcement if state lines hadn't been crossed and FBI jurisdiction if they had.

"We have been retained by the victims' families," Merrigan responded.

"Wait. Families?" he asked.

I turned the page to see there was more than one investigation involved.

"Three?" Again, Onyx asked the same question I wanted to.

"What we believe, is that a serial killer is on the loose. One targeting the daughters of wealthy families in the area."

Targeting daughters of wealthy families? *Fuck.* Maisie fit the victim's profile better than anyone.

At the same time I stood, so did Onyx. I didn't care what anyone thought about us disrupting the meeting; I had to see Maisie with my own eyes and make sure she was next door, talking, laughing, enjoying time with Blanca and my brother.

I went to the kitchen and looked out the window. *"No!"* I shouted when I saw the door to the camp was swinging open. Why was the fucking door open? It was the middle of winter.

I drew my gun as I raced to have my worst fears confirmed. Both Jimmy and Blanca were gagged, blindfolded, and tied to chairs.

"Where the hell is Maisie?" I shouted at Jimmy as Wasp untied him while Onyx did the same with Blanca.

"They took her," Blanca cried as soon as the gag was out of her mouth.

"Who?"

"Two men. Dressed all in black. Ski masks," Jimmy said between gasps of air. "Used tasers."

"He's been hit." Wasp pointed to the blood seeping into the fabric of my brother's shirt. I took a step to the side when Doc rushed over.

"Is there anything else you remember?" I could hear Onyx's words, but they were muffled by the roar of blood surging through my body. Every inch of my skin felt as though it was being pricked by a thousand pins as my brain triggered a fight-or-flight response.

I'd felt it before, more times than I could count, but this was different. This wasn't fear for me. Someone took my *wife*, and it was up to me to find her.

Onyx and I cleared the remaining rooms of the cabin while Doc tended to my brother. At the same time, the rest of the team did a sweep of the property.

"Jimmy suffered a knife wound. I've controlled the bleeding, but I need to get him stitched up. Let's move next door," Doc said when I came back into the cabin's main room.

I got on my brother's uninjured side, and he slung an arm around my shoulders. "I'm sorry, Range. I should've protected her."

"There was nothing you could've done, Jimmy. You were ambushed."

"We need to regroup," I heard Merrigan say while Doc and I got Jimmy into one of the bedrooms. Regroup? As in have a meeting? As in sit on our fucking asses when Maisie had just been abducted? Fuck no. I wouldn't be regrouping.

"How fast can you get a blade?" I asked Wasp.

"I might be able to get someone from forestry to take us up. What do you have in mind?"

"It's the first week of February. How many vehicles are going in and out of the park this time of year? Not to mention, the number of roads that have already been closed cuts down on the area to search."

"And what if she wasn't transported out of the park, Ranger?" Merrigan asked. "She could easily have been taken to one of the other houses on this lake or in the surrounding area."

"I can't sit around and do nothing."

Onyx put his hand on my shoulder. "You know better than this, bro. You're too close, and you need to stand down. If it were me in your shoes right now, you'd tell me to do the same thing."

He had no idea. Would he stand down if it was his wife who had been abducted?

"What's Diesel's twenty?" he asked Doc.

"Ten minutes out."

Onyx turned to me. "We good?"

I gave a head nod. Once Diesel arrived, we would craft our own plan to find Maisie. It's what we did. What we had been doing since our very first mission.

"We're calling in everyone we can, Ranger," said Merrigan, resting her hand on my arm. "You know how vital the first few hours are. We need to start canvassing the area, looking for anyone who might have seen something. What you said about there being fewer people at the lake this time of year will work to our advantage, but we need a plan."

"Canada Lake is a small, tight-knit community. We should be getting the word out, not sitting around here," I muttered under my breath, walking away.

I went to the screened-in porch and looked across the lake to where Maisie's grandparents lived. They needed to know what had happened. I went back inside and through the kitchen to the front door.

"Where are you going?" Onyx asked.

"The Jones' camp."

Instead of trying to talk me out of it, he grabbed the key fob sitting on the kitchen counter. "Let's roll."

"I don't know what I'm going to tell them," I said when he pulled into their driveway.

"You aren't. I am."

"Copy that." If I could speak, I would tell him how much I appreciated him taking charge, but I couldn't. My voice was clogged with emotion.

"You're back! How was your trip?" Mary asked when she opened the door with a big smile on her face. She looked behind me. "Where's Maisie?"

"She isn't with me."

Al put his hand on my beloved wife's grandmother's shoulder, and our eyes met. "What's going on?" he asked.

"Let's go inside and have a seat," said Onyx, leading us all over to the sofa.

"You're scaring me," said Mary. I reached over and covered her hand with mine.

My mind raced as Onyx explained what had gone down in the last couple of hours. If he weren't dead, the first person I'd suspect of taking her was Maxim. I couldn't wrap my head around the fact that it might be the same person who had killed the other three victims. The idea that I'd lose the woman who meant more to me than anyone else before we could even begin our life together sent a frigid chill through my veins.

"We have a team of investigators already here, and more are on their way. Local law enforcement has been called in, as has the FBI. We will do everything we can to find your granddaughter as quickly as possible."

"Who…I mean…why…" Mary broke down, unable to continue.

"We don't know," Onyx answered. "But we're going to find her, Mary."

"The others…" Al began, but couldn't finish.

I'd hoped the Jones hadn't heard about the other kidnappings. Obviously, they had.

"We don't know Maisie's abduction is connected," said Onyx. "We're not ruling it out. We're exploring every possibility."

"I should call Francis," said Al, putting his head in his hands. Francis Arnst was the Jones family's attorney like he'd been our family's since I was a kid. He was an old-school kind of guy—the type where a family didn't make many moves without his advice. It didn't surprise me that Al immediately thought to call him. Francis also represented the three families who had hired our firm to find their daughters' killer.

"Where are Fred and Caroline?" I asked, knowing we'd have to have this conversation a second time with Maisie's mother and father.

"On a cruise somewhere," said Al, looking at his wife.

"Mary, do you know how to reach them?"

"We can try Fred's cell," she said, motioning to her phone on the kitchen counter. Onyx walked over and picked it up.

At the same time, my phone vibrated with an incoming text from Doc Butler. *Diesel and I are headed that way to set up surveillance and communication.*

Copy that, I responded.

"We'll be implementing ways to monitor all incoming calls in the event that whoever took Maisie makes contact," I told them.

"Broad daylight," Al mumbled.

Onyx set the cell phone down and shook his head, indicating he hadn't reached Maisie's parents. "Mary, do you have a list of year-round residents?" he asked.

"Our team will canvas from camp to camp, but knowing which should be occupied will help."

She stood and walked to her desk that looked out over the lake.

I thought about what Merrigan had said earlier about the possibility that Maisie was taken to one of the camps on this very lake. We hadn't gotten far enough in our initial meeting for me to know where the bodies of the other three abducted and subsequently murdered women had been found. I was beginning to regret missing the opportunity to have that, along with other questions I had, answered.

I went to the door when I saw another SUV pull in. Doc and I nodded to each other when he passed by and went inside.

The first thing Diesel and I did was embrace.

"How are you holding up?" he asked.

"I couldn't tell you."

"Understandable."

"Is it?"

"Definitely. Maisie is someone very important to you, and you're a protector."

Important to me? It was so much more than that, but no one knew the extent. Even my best friend in the world.

"It's what you do, Ranger. This is the ultimate test of your abilities. Can you keep your emotions in check in order to save the life of a woman you're in a relationship with?"

Not just a relationship. Maisie was my wife. "How much do you think Doc and Merrigan will actually let me do?"

He shook his head. "It isn't up to them. While they're both under the K19 umbrella, this is a Shadow Ops assignment, not Security Solutions."

"Diesel, what about…" I couldn't bring myself to say the asshole's name.

"Maxim is dead, Range. NYPD confirmed it. We're still waiting for the autopsy results, but they believe the ID is solid."

I nodded, knowing he was right while, at the same time, cursing myself again for refusing to participate in the meeting Merrigan had wanted to have.

I racked my brain, trying to remember what was said before Onyx and I had raced to the cabin next door and discovered Maisie was missing. I'd skimmed a few lines of the report when Merrigan informed us that we'd been retained by the victims' families.

The last words I'd heard before my worst fears were confirmed were that she believed a serial killer was targeting women from wealthy families.

Merrigan was waiting when Diesel, Doc, and I returned to the camp after leaving Mary and Al's place. Onyx had left shortly before we did, saying he'd be with Blanca if we needed him.

"Jimmy is upstairs, resting, but he asked that you wake him when you returned," she said when we came inside.

"Where's everyone else?"

"A command post has been set up at the forestry station on the other side of the lake."

The place had a least ten cabins along with a main lodge, so it was a good place to set something like that up. I pulled out the brief to reread it.

"Money McTiernan is also sending a unit from the agency," I heard Doc say.

"Copy that," I muttered without looking up from the brief.

While the previous kidnappings had taken place within the Adirondack Park boundaries, it wasn't a small area. It encompassed close to six million acres—greater than Yellowstone, the Everglades, Glacier National Park, and Grand Canyon National Park combined, and sixty percent of the park was forested.

The first victim was abducted near Lake Placid. Her body was found over one hundred miles from there. The second was kidnapped near Peck Lake. Her body was discovered in the forest, a five-minute walk from her family's camp. The third was recovered ten miles from where she was taken.

So, no set pattern. Nothing to go on. At least not yet. As Diesel had said, this is what we did. We were protectors, rescuers. We'd gone in and extracted both operatives and civilians from the deadliest of situations. We could do this. We'd find Maisie, then annihilate whoever had taken her.

Something about the way she was kidnapped didn't make sense, though. Blanca and Jimmy had said there were two men. While the brief Merrigan had prepared contained no information about the way the other three women had been abducted, there were few instances I could recall when a serial killer didn't act alone.

"We need to separate from the group and make our own plan," I said quietly enough that I didn't think anyone else had heard me.

"Not without me, you won't." I hadn't seen Onyx come in, and it was obvious Diesel hadn't either.

I flexed both my hands and looked over to where Doc stood talking with Merrigan. "Where are they staying?"

"At the forestry lodge," Onyx answered. "We'll wait until they head out to talk, then we'll join them to outline the steps we intend to take."

I nodded. "Who is with Blanca?"

"Swan on the inside. Buster and Wasp watching the outer perimeter." Onyx put his hand on my shoulder. "This is K19 Shadow Ops' first official mission, and while I hate with every fiber of my being that it's to find Maisie, you know as well as I do that *we will not fail*."

I prayed he was right.

Merrigan walked over and embraced me. "Is there anything else you need from us right now?"

Onyx answered for me. "Give us a few minutes, and we'll be right behind you."

"Copy that," said Doc, answering for them both.

Once we saw them drive away, the three of us gathered around the kitchen island. Diesel pulled out a map of the Adirondack Park. He'd obviously had the same line of thinking I had because I saw he'd circled the areas where the other women had been abducted and also where they were found.

"No pattern," muttered Onyx, also reiterating my earlier thoughts.

"We should have video footage from every route leading out of the park within a few hours," said Diesel. "Money has the agency pulling from every business as well as forestry service cams."

Given how undeveloped most of the park was, the latter would give us the most information, but I didn't hold out a lot of hope that whoever had taken Maisie would have transported her in plain view. God, I felt so powerless. I couldn't spend another minute doing nothing.

"I'm ready to start canvassing camps now. I don't need another fucking meeting."

Onyx looked at Diesel before looking at me. "I want you to take a step back from this."

When I stood, the stool I'd been sitting on crashed to the floor. "I don't give a fuck what you want. I'll do this on my own—"

"Look, I know you're upset—"

I interrupted Onyx like he had me. "*Upset? Did you say upset? I'm not fucking upset. I feel like there's a part of me dying inside, and I cannot let it. Do you understand? I can't let it.*"

"I understand how much Maisie means to you—"

"You don't have a fucking clue how much she means to me. Maisie is the love of my life." I nearly broke down, but I had to get the next words out. *"She's my wife."*

The emotion I'd been holding inside erupted out of me like a volcano. "She's my wife," I repeated, this time with tears in my eyes. "She's my fucking wife."

Both Onyx and Diesel stood. "I'm sorry, Range. I had no idea. Although it makes sense now that you've said it. I should've realized. That's why we had to stand down at Long Lake."

I nodded. "We got married that night."

My eyes met Onyx's. His were filled with tears like mine were. "We will find her and bring her back safe."

"To God's ears," I muttered, rubbing my chest.

18

Maisie

Where in the hell was I, and what was wrong with my body? It was as though no matter how hard I tried to open my eyes, they just wouldn't. My arms and legs wouldn't move either.

I could hear music from the carousel, faintly, unless it was just another of the strange dreams I'd been having. The sound of it usually soothed me, but not now. Now, it was more as if the music was distorted, like a special effect in a horror movie. It made me sad, not that my eyes would shed tears any more than they'd open.

My family's amusement park had been my refuge when I was growing up. My grandparents ran it then. Not anymore, though. It had been closed for years, but I was trying to change that. But how? I couldn't remember, just like I couldn't open my eyes or move my arms. I drifted back to sleep and to the dream that played over and over in my head. It was about Ranger on the first day we met. It was years ago, but it felt as though it had happened yesterday.

I'd been working the docks at the Canada Lake Store when he pulled his family's Chris-Craft up to fill the gas tank.

"What's the tab under?" I'd asked, surprising myself with how nonchalant my voice sounded, given my insides were doing somersaults in the insanely handsome boy's presence. His dark-brown hair curled where it touched his ears, and his warm whiskey-colored eyes took in the other boats moored at the dock. I didn't dare look down at his bare chest, already tanned even though the summer season had just begun.

"Messick," he said without even looking at me. Why would he have? I was a gangling fourteen-year-old with white-blonde hair, pale skin, and long legs that made me look like a foal trying to stand after just being birthed.

"I can get it," he said, brushing my hand with his for a split second before trying to take the nozzle from me.

"We're not allowed to let customers pump their own gas."

"What about other employees?"

I shrugged. "Of course other employees can."

"Then, gimme that." He put one hand on my arm and took the nozzle with the other. "I'm Owen, and I start tomorrow."

"Maisie Ann," I said, wishing I'd left off my middle name. It made me sound like the kid I was.

"Maisie Ann," he repeated. "I like it."

"Did you know Jimmy Messick has a younger brother?" I asked my friend Jill when she joined me down on the docks at the start of her shift.

"Owen? Oh, yeah."

"How do you know him?"

"He plays basketball with my older brother."

I never missed a basketball game after that. Or baseball when I learned he played that sport too.

I saw him more during the summer, though, when the kids from the camps around the lake would meet up at Nick Stoner Island. We'd all pile into boats and motor to the spit of land in the middle of the lake, where we'd have a bonfire, drink beer, and hang out. Once in a while, we'd see a couple sneak off to the other side of the island to make out.

Never me, though. I remained the ugly duckling until the summer between my junior and senior year of high school.

By then, Owen Messick, whom I heard the gang had started calling Ranger, wasn't at the lake that often. He'd come up for an occasional weekend and I might catch a glimpse of him at the lake store, but he never acted like he recognized me.

At least not until the night of my eighteenth birthday.

***

A loud noise jarred me from the dream, and I was able to open one eye only to realize I'd been blindfolded. As feeling in my extremities and control over my muscles returned, so did my short-term memory.

First, I'd been tased, then I'd watched in horror as a man wearing a mask and gloves injected something into my leg. After that, I didn't remember a thing.

I tried to move my arms, but they were bound. My legs were too, and I had a gag in my mouth. While I was wrapped in a coarse blanket, underneath, I was naked.

"Ah, the princess has finally awoken." The voice of the person speaking sounded familiar, but it made no sense.

The man covered my body with his, pressing his hardness against me. I wanted to puke as he unwrapped the blanket and his lips moved from my neck down to my bare breasts.

"Don't touch me!" I attempted to scream through the gag, but the words were unintelligible. He flipped me to my stomach and pressed my face into the hard ground beneath the blanket.

When I felt him fumbling with his zipper, I closed my eyes as tight as I could and pulled my knees up, bucking my body.

"You fucking bitch." He grabbed my hair and pulled my head back. His mouth was next to my ear, and he bit the lobe hard enough that I screamed again through the gag. He sat up, straddling my waist. Seconds later, I felt the pinch of the needle in my thigh, and everything faded to black.

19

Ranger

"Who in the hell is that?" I asked Onyx when we walked into the main lodge of the forestry camp and I saw a woman I didn't recognize.

His fists clenched. "No idea, but we're about to find out."

Diesel grabbed his arm before he could stalk over to where the stranger stood talking with Doc and Merrigan. "That's Special Agent Bryar Davies. The FBI sent her in."

"Why am I just learning about this now?" Onyx said under his breath.

When Diesel held up his phone, Onyx looked at his. "Got it."

Maybe I'd received a text about it too, but I didn't give a shit. I wanted this meeting over so we could start doing something rather than just talk about it. It was almost midnight, and Maisie had been abducted at nine this morning. Fifteen hours, and as far as I knew, we had no leads regarding her whereabouts.

Onyx introduced himself to the FBI agent, introduced me, then turned to Diesel.

"Agent Davies, Mr. Jacks will be your point person for this investigation."

Diesel held out his hand, but Ms. Davies—in her late twenties at the most—didn't shake it.

"This is FBI jurisdiction. If there are assignments to be made, I will be the one making them."

"Like I said, if you have any questions, Diesel will be the one to answer them." He turned to walk away, but stopped and looked over his shoulder. "And that's only if I decide you need to know."

"But—"

"Doc, Merrigan, a word." Onyx motioned to me. I followed them into a separate room and closed the door behind me. "There's been a development Ranger needs to share with you."

They turned to me.

"Maisie and I are married."

Doc's eyes met Merrigan's, and she nodded. "We know, Ranger."

I didn't bother to ask how. It didn't matter. "If you think I'm going to stand down—"

Merrigan put her hand on my arm. "We would suggest nothing of the kind, and even if we did, Onyx would never agree. However, there are certain protocols that need to be followed for kidnapping cases."

"Such as?"

"We will take a look at what Agent Davies has prepared, as well as what you've done." She looked between Onyx and me, and neither of us contradicted her.

"Then, we'll begin."

"Roger that," said Onyx at the same time I did.

"Ranger, a word?" asked Doc. "You need to get some rest. Either here or at your camp. I know it's the last thing you want to do, but you'll need to be full bore in the morning."

Before I could respond, there was a knock at the door and Diesel came in. "I'm sorry to interrupt, but this can't wait."

"What is it?" asked Doc.

"A ransom request has come in."

We raced over to one of the guys I knew from the agency who was setting up the recording for us to hear. Unsurprisingly, the speaker's voice had been digitally distorted. The caller requested twenty million dollars be delivered in two separate drops of ten million each. Both were fairly public locations: one in Gloversville and one in Johnstown, the two biggest cities in the vicinity of Canada Lake.

It was a common tactic, seen most often in movies or on TV. The idea was that the kidnapper could surveil the first drop to see if the person who picked up the bag was being followed. If not, the rest would be safe to collect. It rarely worked in real life, which meant our kidnapper wasn't as experienced as we'd initially believed.

Agent Davies shook her head while listening. "The amount of the demand as well as the requested delivery is different. I anticipate we'll hear from him sooner rather than later since he gave no time frame."

"Francis Arnst is here with Al and Mary now," reported Buster, who was inside their camp when the ransom call came in.

"When did he arrive?" I asked.

"Al contacted him yesterday and asked for a meeting this morning. Mr. Arnst is helping them put the ransom together."

I nodded, then motioned Diesel off to the side of the room. "See what you can find out about the previous abduction details, specifically if there are reports of more than one assailant."

"Roger that."

He was only gone a couple of minutes when he walked back over to where I was talking with Doc, Merrigan, and Onyx. "*Nada.* Nothing on the abductions themselves."

My eyes met Onyx's. There had to have been some evidence, but given the length of time that had passed, it was too late to look for things like footprints.

"Is there any connection between the three previous victims outside of them being from wealthy families who lived inside park boundaries?"

"I believe Money has someone at the CIA working on that."

"Actually, the FBI discovered a connection," said Agent Davies, who stood over us with her arms folded.

"And?"

"All four, including the latest victim, went to college in close proximity to Hanover, New Hampshire."

"Dartmouth," I said under my breath.

"Yes, two of them were Dartmouth grads, one went to Lebanon College, and the fourth to Plymouth State University."

I didn't like this connection one bit, and looking at Diesel, I could tell he didn't either.

When I went outside, he followed. "Anything from the coroner?" I asked.

"Not yet."

The door opened, and Onyx joined us. "You keep forgetting to invite me to participate in your conversations. Now, fill me in on why you had to come out here to talk."

I gave him the shortest version I could of Maxim Edwards' story.

"Buster was on his detail."

"That's right."

"Are you under the impression the rest of the team neglects to share information with me in the same way either of you do?" I'd rarely seen Onyx as angry as he was presently. "I understand the two of you are used to crafting your own plans, operating outside of the team, but the three of us *are* the team."

"I apologize, but—"

"As soon as you add that word, it's not an apology; it's an excuse."

"Yes, sir."

"Diesel, you get in there and brief Agent Davies. Ranger, you and I are gonna stay out here and talk." Rather than saying anything to me, Onyx pulled out his phone and placed a call.

"Rock, I've got a situation with the serial killer investigation."

Ritter "Rock" Johnson was another guy I knew from my days with the CIA. Last I heard, he was still with them.

I continued listening to Onyx's side of the conversation. "I need you to press the coroner for results on the death of Maxim Edwards." He ended the call and stuck his phone back in his pocket.

"What else?"

"Why did the charges against him disappear?"

"Fill me in."

"Edwards was being investigated for multiple counts of securities fraud. He was about to be indicted, and suddenly, the whole thing went away."

He rubbed his jaw. "I don't have connections to anyone in the New York Attorney General's office. Let's see who does."

"What's happening with the ransom demand?"

"Doc is handling it. He and Merrigan left a few minutes ago for the Jones' camp."

When I turned to go inside, Onyx asked me to wait.

"Listen, I get that it's damn hard to sit on your hands, but I'm asking you to anyway. Teams were out checking camps earlier and will resume in the morning. The CIA and FBI are both working this from different directions. For this investigation and every one that comes after it, you lead, Ranger. That's your job."

"Would it be that easy for you?"

His eyes bored into mine. "Sure as shit not. However, we've worked how many missions together?"

I shook my head.

"Let me ask you this. How would they have gone down if our team leaders didn't let us do our jobs? What if they believed they were the only ones who could?"

When we went inside, Diesel was headed our way, phone in hand. "The ID was wrong on Maxim Edwards."

"Fuck!" I spat. "Do they know who *was* murdered?"

"Not yet. The DNA was a match, but not exact. Whoever it is, was a close relative. They're working on fingerprints now. So far, no match has come up."

"Which is how they knew it wasn't Maxim." He'd been printed when he was charged. "What about dental records?"

Diesel shook his head. "They weren't left with much to go on."

"More importantly, Edwards isn't dead. Combine that with the connection to Dartmouth and other colleges in the surrounding area, and we have ourselves a suspect."

20

Maisie

Without any way to calculate the passage of time, I had no idea how long I'd been kept in a drug-induced state. It could've been hours or days.

When he thought I was awake, the man holding me would either slap me around, bite different parts of my body, or pull my hair as he spat in my face. He would press my body into the dirt, and I could feel him trying to push his penis inside me. Each time, before I knew whether he'd succeeded in raping me, he'd inject me with more drugs that made me lose consciousness again.

Since the first time, when he'd called me princess, the man hadn't spoken. He also hadn't fed me or given me anything to drink that I remembered. I also couldn't remember how many times I'd woken up only to be reinjected.

I hadn't heard the carousel again; maybe it had been a dream after all. There was something familiar about the smell of wherever I was being held, but even if I could remain awake long enough to figure out where it was, I had no way to tell anyone.

I knew I dreamed, mostly about Ranger. For the brief periods I was awake, I thought only of him. I knew he would be looking for me, and that was the only thing giving me hope I'd make it out of here alive.

I couldn't allow myself to think of what might happen then. The horror of what I was going through was bad enough. Wondering if Ranger would still want me after I'd been raped was not something I could handle now.

Maybe the man knew how long the drugs would keep me unconscious because it always seemed that within minutes, he'd slam the door open and get close enough to me that I could smell his breath.

"You are more valued than I thought," said the voice that reminded me so much of Maxim's. But it couldn't be. Maxim was dead. Wasn't he? Had I dreamed Ranger telling me he was? "Only a few more hours until I get the money that will allow us to disappear forever."

Us? Had he said us? And was he referring to me disappearing with him or someone else after they killed me? Or left me here to die.

21

Ranger

Given Buster and his crew, who had been tasked with surveilling him, believed Edwards had been in his apartment in New York City, he must've known a way out we didn't.

Someone was pulling motor vehicle records so we could put an alert out for any he owned. Once those came in, the agent responsible for scouring video surveillance would have something specific to start looking for.

The most obvious witnesses of the abduction were Al and Mary since they could see my camp from theirs. However, they were grocery shopping in Johnstown when the kidnapping took place. The rest of the neighboring camps, besides the ones my teammates were occupying, were boarded up for the winter.

Finding a vehicle that may have been used to transport Maisie was our best hope, for the time being.

I understood what Doc had said about me being full bore in the morning, but that didn't mean my brain would shut down enough to allow me to rest.

I looked across the room to where Diesel and the FBI agent were head-to-head. Something about the woman rubbed me the wrong way. Maybe it was her "outsider" status. While I didn't personally know everyone Money McTiernan had sent up from the agency, I knew their names and what part of the agency they worked for.

As far as local law enforcement, I'd known the majority of the deputies and the sheriff since I was a kid. Canada Lake wasn't the kind of place someone transferred to in order to advance their career. Those who worked locally did so because this was their home.

That left Agent Davies. To me, she looked like a kid. Too green to really help us. Was I being fair, though? Wasn't she around Maisie's age? And that was only four years younger than me.

I'd wanted to throttle Edwards when he suggested Maisie didn't have the experience to pull off her plans for Canada Lake's redevelopment. I was making the same assumption about Davies.

However, judging by the scowl on his face when Diesel abruptly left their conversation, I wondered if I was right about her.

Doc and Merrigan walked into the lodge. Both looked haggard.

"What's the status of the ransom payment?" I asked.

Merrigan sighed and looked at her husband.

"The attorney is pressing them to pay as soon as the bank can free up the cash, which would be sometime tomorrow afternoon." He looked at his watch. "Or I should say this afternoon."

"Are you suggesting they don't pay it?"

Doc shook his head. "I can't tell them not to do everything they can to get their granddaughter back. However, the three previous victims were killed despite the ransom being paid. So far, there is no trace of that money being used anywhere."

Doc's words about the other victims being killed were like a stab to my heart. He was right, though, as hard as it was to hear.

"We're going to call it a night," he said, putting his arm around Merrigan's shoulders. "If anything significant comes up, call my cell. I'll only be a few steps away. By the way, Ranger, there's a room set up for you too. Even if you can't sleep, try to get some rest."

"Where?"

Merrigan pulled out a key card and handed it to me. "Number seven. It's right next to ours."

"Thanks."

I went in search of Diesel and found him outside. "What's going on?"

He looked up at the sky. "Thinking the same things you are, Range. I want to find her." He rubbed his eyes. "The FBI has drones up now, checking all the camps that aren't supposed to be occupied."

"You and the agent don't appear to see eye to eye."

"If that isn't the understatement of the fucking century," he muttered. "The thing is, she's smart. Damn smart. So as much as I might want to discredit her, I can't. We're lucky to have her on this investigation."

"I came out to tell you I'm going to lie down in one of the rooms in the lodge. If you need me, I'll be in number seven."

"Copy that."

When I went inside, the agent was stretching. "Do you have a place to get some rest?" I asked, attempting to offer an olive branch of sorts.

"I'm monitoring the drones presently, but after that, I'll take a break. Oh, and to answer your question, I'm in one of the cabins."

I nodded and walked in the direction of the hallway where the rooms were located and bumped into Onyx coming out of one.

"Why didn't you go back to Blanca's camp?"

"I did. I brought her here so we wouldn't use assets we need here, there to keep an eye on her."

"Thanks, Onyx."

"We're going to find Maisie and bring her back safe. We aren't at the twenty-four-hour mark yet."

"Copy that," I mumbled as I walked to my room. I wasn't there more than thirty minutes before Diesel pounded on my door.

"We've got a hit on the car and are sending a drone to detect whether someone is in the vicinity," he said when I motioned for him to come in.

"Where is it?"

"Sherman's."

I hadn't bothered to take off my clothes before I lay down, so I pushed past him.

"What have you got?" I asked Agent Davies.

"A few more seconds, and I'll be able to tell you."

"We need to assemble a team."

"On it," Onyx shouted over to me while I watched the agent's laptop for signs the drone had detected life.

"They're there," she announced, looking up at me. I studied the screen a few seconds more to see how many people were, based on the drone's detection of movement. *Three.*

"Let's move out!" I shouted.

Doc came out of the hallway, carrying two sets of tactical gear and tossed one to me. "Suit up."

I did and raced out the door to a waiting SUV with the engine running and the front passenger door open. Diesel was behind the wheel.

We had two hours before the sun rose, taking away the advantage we had with the NVDs, but I didn't need to tell him to hurry. My best guess was he was doing at least ninety once we got out on the road. He'd probably been going sixty on the gravel drive of the forestry camp.

Onyx sent a text showing the setup of where everyone would be going in and who was on each team. I was leading the one closest to where the drone had picked up signs of life. Onyx, Diesel, Wasp, and Buster were going in with me.

This was something we'd done countless times in situations far more dangerous than this one. Ones where we were outnumbered ten or more to one. In all the years I'd been doing extractions, I hadn't lost a single target. I wouldn't today, either.

"When we're in, we'll take out Edwards and whoever else is with him while you get Maisie," said Onyx.

Take him out. That's right. The motherfucker would take his last breath in a matter of minutes. But what if there were other victims we didn't know about?

"Keep him alive if at all possible," I said through the mic. We'd interrogate the fuck out of the *sonuvabitch* until we got our answers. After that—we'd see.

"Roger that," Onyx and Diesel responded.

We entered the bathhouse but stayed on the building's interior perimeter. The drone had picked up breathing near the center of the structure on a lower level. I couldn't remember ever seeing an entrance leading to a basement, but there had to be one somewhere. After five minutes, we hadn't found one.

"Agent Davies, contact Al Jones and ask him how to access the bathhouse basement," I said into the mic. He'd know, and it would save time.

"Roger that."

We waited for her reply, staying as stealthy as possible. What felt like an hour but was only minutes later, I heard her voice.

"There isn't one from the bathhouse. There's a tunnel you can access from the carousel. It goes under the midway. There is no other way in or out except via that access point. He said there used to be an entrance from the building above it, but the fire department made him drywall over it."

"Copy that. Let's move."

We filed out, and when my team went to the left, team two went to the right. Team three went around by the lakefront. The fourth and final team was in position between the bathhouse, the length of the midway, and the parking lot. I heard Onyx tell them to stay put.

Once we located the trapdoor, I went in first. Through my NVDs, I could see signs of recent footprints. Two sets.

I raced through the tunnels, counting the steps that I had taken when we left the bathhouse. I was about to round a corner when I heard a noise in front of me. It sounded like someone cocking a gun. I motioned for the guys behind me to slow and get down. I aimed my firearm in the direction I'd heard the noise, hoping the NVDs gave me an advantage over whoever was about to shoot at me. I stuck my head around the corner and fired at the same time he did.

He missed. I didn't. Not with the first or second shot I got off.

Diesel came up directly behind me and trained his gun on the guy we both believed was dead. I raced past him and rounded another corner. There, I saw a door. It was the first we'd come to.

I moved into position at the left side of it, Buster was on the right, and Onyx kicked it in. I followed them in; Wasp was right behind me.

I saw the outline of a body, too big to be Maisie, who appeared to be asleep on a cot. Onyx and Buster woke him by shoving the barrel of a gun into his side and against his head.

Beyond him was a second door. I raced toward it, more terrified of what I'd find than I had been during any other extraction. I kicked it open and saw Maisie's body on the floor, wrapped in a blanket. I rushed to her and checked for a pulse. She was warm and breathing, thank God, but even through the limited light of the NVD, I could see she'd been roughed up. When I gathered her into my arms, the blanket fell open. She was naked underneath.

"I've got her," I said into the mic. "Doc, what's your twenty?"

"In the tunnel, headed your way."

Doc was given his code name because he was a physician's assistant—one of the best I'd ever worked with. We needed to add one to the Shadow Ops team before our next mission. The role was a vital one.

We met near the tunnel's exit. "Her breathing is shallow, pulse weak, and she hasn't come to."

"Copy that. Let's get her out of here so I can take a look. There's a bus on its way."

I saw the paramedics pull up to the carousel entrance when I came out of the trapdoor. I rushed toward them at the same time they lowered a stretcher, and I took a step back when Doc reiterated what I'd said about her pulse and breathing.

"Get in, Ranger," said Doc.

"Sir, we don't allow—"

"He's riding in the back with me." I'd known Doc a long time, but when he used that tone of voice, he intimidated the hell out of me. The EMT looked like Zeus had just rained his wrath down on him.

"Yes, sir."

Doc and I removed Maisie's blindfold, the gag in her mouth, and untied her arms and legs. When the EMT got out two other blankets, I put one over her, removed what had been wrapped around her, and tossed it to Diesel. "Bag it."

"Roger that."

I put the second blanket over her and held Maisie's hand as the driver sped toward Johnstown and the nearest hospital. We were five minutes out when her eyes opened and she looked into mine.

"Hey, beautiful," I said, bringing her hand to my mouth so I could kiss the back of it.

"Ranger?" Her voice was hoarse.

"I'm right here, Maisie."

"What happened?"

"You were lost, but I found you."

"He…he…" She closed her eyes, and I stroked her hair.

"It's over. You're safe," I whispered.

When she started to tremble, I got on my knees and wrapped my arms around her.

"You stay with Maisie. I'll head in and talk to the triage team," Doc said when we pulled up to the hospital's emergency room.

I moved out of the way while the EMTs eased the stretcher from the back of the ambulance and wheeled her inside. Doc had a medical team ready and waiting in a bay to evaluate her condition.

He put his hand on my arm and motioned for me to follow. When we were a few feet away from where Maisie was being examined, he turned to look at me. "I've suggested a tox screen as well as a rape kit."

The words were like a punch to my gut, but I knew they were as necessary as evaluating the rest of the injuries she'd sustained. "Edwards?" I asked.

"In custody."

"Whose and where?"

"Ours, and that information is need-to-know."

"I'm the one who asked he be kept alive. I'm not going to kill him—yet."

"Understood. Trust when I say the Shadow Ops team will get every ounce of information they want out of him."

I knew they would, especially with Onyx's and Diesel's participation.

"What about the other guy?"

"Dead and yet to be identified."

I looked back to the doctors and nurses who were tending to my wife.

"She's in good hands," said Doc. "And she's alive."

"I know. I just need to be with her."

A woman carrying a clipboard approached us. "Are you Mrs. Messick's husband?"

"I am."

"I just need you to sign a couple of these forms, giving us permission to examine her and run the necessary tests."

I scrawled my name where she pointed.

"Maisie may have issues with memory," said Doc when she walked away. "We'll know how much to anticipate once the initial toxicology report comes in. We'll take it slow, not force her to talk about anything she isn't ready to."

"Has someone contacted Al and Mary?"

"Merrigan is bringing them here now."

"Thanks, Doc, for everything."

"It's what we do, Ranger, and you're welcome."

22

Ranger

As soon as Doc and I finished talking, I rushed back to the bay where Maisie was being examined. She'd already had too many strangers' hands on her, from Doc to the EMTs, and now the doctors and nurses. I didn't want her to face anyone else without me by her side.

When I walked in, Maisie turned her head in the direction of the doctor who was entering notes into a computer. It seemed odd. I expected her to reach out to me, at least look at me, but she didn't. I pulled a chair closer to the gurney and attempted to take her hand, but she moved it out of my reach.

Rather than doing anything to make her more uncomfortable, I leaned back in the chair and waited for the doctor to finish his notes.

He closed the laptop and bent over the bed rail. "We'll start an IV to replenish your fluids. I'll be back in an hour to see how you're doing," was all he said.

Maisie nodded and the man left. Rather than rush after him for an update on her condition, I walked around to the other side of the bed so I could see her face. "Hey, there," I said, brushing her hair from her forehead. She flinched.

I stood by the bed, watching after she closed her eyes. She needed rest—God knew what kind of drugs were in her system.

I sat in a chair, checking messages and emails until I nodded off like she had. I woke when I felt someone's hand on my shoulder. I turned my head and looked up at Doc, who motioned for me to follow.

I was about to say I didn't want to leave Maisie alone when Swan arrived and waited for me to vacate the chair so she could be seated. A nurse also came in to start the IV.

Doc led me into a room with a sofa, two chairs, and a side table. He closed the door behind us. "Have a seat."

I did and leaned forward with my elbows on my knees.

"What I have to tell you is going to be very difficult for you to hear, Ranger. Although, I doubt it will come as a surprise."

I brought my hands to my face. "Go ahead."

"Maisie was repeatedly raped both vaginally and anally. She suffered several lacerations, which resulted in bleeding, and there were minor tears in her posterior fourchette. Based on her bruising, it appears she was struck several times and suffered abrasions over the majority of her body."

I knew Doc was doing everything in his power to be straightforward and informative, but it was all I could do not to race from the room and puke.

"We were able to collect semen samples. At the minimum, it will serve as evidence. It's hard to say how much Maisie will recollect. We'll know more once we get the results of the tox screen."

"Wherever the motherfucker is, make sure I can't find him."

"Understood."

"Is there more you're not saying?"

"Again, until the tox results come in, there isn't much more I *can* say."

"She's withdrawn." When Doc didn't respond, I looked at him. "From me."

Doc leaned forward. "It's to be expected."

"I don't know what to do."

"There's literature available for partners of survivors of sexual assault. There are also on-staff psychologists available to help you through some of this."

I knew Doc's first wife, not Merrigan, had been a sexual assault survivor. It had happened over twenty years ago. "How did you handle it?"

He rubbed the back of his neck. "Not as well as I should have."

I'd much rather have this conversation with him—a man who was like an older brother to me, a mentor—than a stranger whose approach would be clinical. "What can you share with me?"

"Much of this is in the literature the hospital provides, but I'll go over it with you if it would help."

"It would."

"First and foremost, don't pressure Maisie to talk. Let her set the pace."

"Makes sense."

"Next, don't blame yourself. For you, this may be the most difficult part. 'If you hadn't left Maisie alone to attend our meeting, none of this would have happened.'"

I didn't respond, but it was the absolute truth.

"Know that Maisie is going to blame herself too, but that isn't something you can address with her until she talks to you about it. Just because you *know* that's what she's doing doesn't give you an open door to try to get her to talk about it."

"That's gonna be hard."

"Damn right, it is. All of it will be, Ranger. This is why you have to make sure you have a support system. Not just a support system for Maisie—one for you too."

"I don't want her to pull farther away from me."

"Of course you don't. You want to be right by her side, believing you're helping her. Try to remember you might not be."

I stood and paced the room.

"Talk to the psychologist, Ranger. Today. Don't wait. Don't tell yourself you have to take care of Maisie first. Until you get the support you need, you may not be able to help her at all. Remember, she needs to be in control of her own life."

That, I understood. Maxim Edwards took away her power along with her control. She was one of the smartest, most capable women I knew. I prayed she remembered that, found her way back to that, without pressure from me.

"I said that you not blaming yourself might be the most difficult part for you. I spoke too soon. Intimacy may be the hardest part to work your way through. Maisie may feel very differently about sex, and it may take a long time for her to feel as though she can interact with you sexually."

I thought about every conversation she and I had had about how jealous I got when I thought about her being with other men. I wished I could take it all back. Every word. Who knew what kind of irreparable damage I may have inadvertently done by being an immature asshole.

"But also remember, what Edwards did to her wasn't a sexual act. It was one of violence."

"I understand."

"Finally, all you can really do is be patient and open to communication. Create a safe place for her to talk or not talk, deal or not deal, even pretend it never happened. Whatever she needs to do to get through this, make it all okay. I can't tell you how much I wish I'd done that for my ex-wife."

"Thanks, Doc."

"I'm available any time, day or night, whatever you need, Ranger. I'm *your* safe place. I hope you know that."

"I do."

"Help me help you by talking to this psychologist."

"I will."

"Today."

"Roger that."

When I returned to the emergency room bay, Al and Mary were with Maisie, so I walked over to the desk and requested the contact information for the psychologist.

"Would you like me to schedule an appointment for you?" the nurse behind the counter asked.

"Sure. I mean, I guess so."

She typed something on the computer, then stared at the screen. "She has an opening at two, three, and four."

"Today?"

The woman looked up at me. "Yes. Today. It's always best if Ms. Fasano is able to meet with family members as soon after the assault as possible."

"What about the victim?"

"I believe she's already spoken with your wife, sir."

"When?"

"I don't know, but did you want me to set something up for this afternoon?"

"Two." The sooner, the better. Maybe then I could get some answers about why this woman had taken it upon herself to meet with Maisie without my knowing about it.

The nurse handed me a card. "With patients, she will typically come to the room. With family members, it's best to meet in her office. It's on the third floor."

"Do you know if my wife will be going home this afternoon or if the plan is to admit her?"

"I can't answer that, but I'll find someone who can."

23

Maisie

My head throbbed. It was the only way I knew I was actually inside my body. I hurt. Otherwise, I felt like a spectator, looking at myself from somewhere else. Not here. Not even in this room. Just watching from afar. Wondering how the fuck I got here.

I wasn't conscious when I was rescued from my worst nightmare. Was the piece of shit who put me there dead? God, I hoped so. Or did I hope he was alive, living his own version of the torment he'd forced on me? No, I wanted him dead. Then he'd be in the bowels of hell, being endlessly tortured, suffering horrific pain for all eternity. That's what I hoped the most.

My grandmother's hands shook when she tried to get me to drink some water. I could barely get my lips around the straw because it was moving around so much. "I'm sorry," I heard her whisper.

No! I wanted to scream. *Don't you dare be sorry!* Don't be sorry about your shaking hands. Don't be sorry I was kidnapped. Don't be sorry the man I once thought I worshiped had violated my body in unimaginable ways. Don't be *sorry* for any of it. And don't fucking feel sorry for me. I wanted no pity. Especially from her. Especially from Ranger.

If Maxim had given me even the smallest window of opportunity, I would've cut off his dick and choked him with it.

Instead, he'd used drugs to incapacitate me. I knew he'd raped me, but not because I remembered it. He was too much of a coward to do it while I was lucid. Perhaps afraid of what he might see in my eyes if he had. Instead, I knew because of the examination I'd had to endure when I first arrived at the hospital. Thank God I was still half out of it then.

I hadn't been able to look at Ranger earlier. I wasn't sure I could now. I couldn't look at Grandpa Al either. I knew he'd be blaming himself. The pain of not protecting me would chew him up. He'd cry, and I couldn't handle that.

My grandmother was shaky, but that was nerves. She needed a glass of sherry to calm herself. After two, she'd be as fighting mad as I was. Better able to channel all her worry into something that looked more like revenge.

But that wouldn't be good either. What was the expression? Revenge is like taking poison and waiting for the other person to die. No, not revenge.

"Maisie?"

I couldn't look at her face.

I closed my eyes when she cupped my cheek. "Yeah, Grandma?"

"I love you so."

Not the words I expected, which meant I wasn't prepared for them. Instead of being able to keep my anger close, like a shield, her love for me shattered it. I could feel a sob welling deep in my chest, fighting its way out of my body. No matter how hard I tried, I couldn't swallow it back down. It came tearing out of me like a gale—a howl more than a wail—and yet, almost silent. My body closed in on itself as the pain poured out of me. I wrapped my arms around my stomach and held as tight as I could.

Grandma Mary tried to embrace me, surround me in her arms, but they weren't long enough.

My grandfather came around the other side, and between the two of them, they formed a cocoon of protective insulation. Except the pain was coming from the inside. They weren't keeping it away; they were holding it in.

"No," I pleaded, wriggling out of their embrace.

"Maisie?"

I opened my eyes and saw Ranger standing in front of me. I couldn't read his expression, but I knew it wasn't pity. My grandmother moved out of his way when he took a step toward the gurney.

"Leave us," I heard him plead as he gathered me in his arms. We lay on the small space, my back to his front so the pain had a way to get out. Out of me, but not into him.

I could feel his power, his strength. He wasn't weak from his inability to keep me safe. I didn't feel him punishing himself. I felt him protecting me.

24

Ranger

I knew the moment Maisie let me in. I felt it in the way her body melded into mine. Part of me feared it wouldn't happen, but as soon as I witnessed her suffering, I knew I was the only person who could be strong in the way she needed me to be.

No doubt. No questions. No judgment. No pressure. Just strength. Wherever and however she needed it. Maisie was mine and I was hers. Nothing could ever change that. Nothing.

I smoothed her hair back, sweaty from expelling the pain from her body. It wasn't all gone. It never would be. The memories of the last several hours would be ingrained in her until the day she died. Her life had changed. From now on, it would be divided into two halves. It would be her decision—and mine—how those halves were defined. Before the abduction and after? Or before we fell in love and after we committed our lives to each other? More than lives, my soul belonged to Maisie, and hers belonged to me. Nothing would ever change that. I wouldn't let it.

I'd witnessed inconceivable suffering in the course of my career. I'd seen men die in unimaginably horrific ways. I'd also seen them live to overcome what hadn't killed them.

Maisie was alive. That's all that mattered. She would overcome what hadn't killed her, and I'd be by her side for every step she took. If she fell, I'd pick her up. If she quit, I'd help her start again the next day.

I kissed her temple and said the only words that mattered. "I love you, Maisie Ann Messick."

Her response was so quiet, I had to hold my breath to hear it. "I love you too."

I had no delusions that the days, weeks, months, even years ahead of us would be easy. We'd still walk into every sunrise with the hope each new day brought.

Maisie turned in my arms and buried her face in my chest. Her fingernails dug into my skin through the fabric of my shirt. I wrapped my arm around her waist and pulled her body closer to mine. "I love you," I repeated.

She didn't respond this time, but I didn't need to hear the words. I knew she loved me too.

I opened my eyes when I heard a man clear his throat.

"We're going to admit your wife overnight," said the doctor I recognized from earlier. "At least until we have the toxicology report back and know what's in her system."

"Understood." I waited for him to make a comment about me being on the gurney with her, but he didn't.

"Someone will be in shortly to take her up to a room."

"Thank you."

I glanced at the clock, grateful I didn't need to meet with the psychologist for another four hours.

My cell vibrated, but I didn't take it out of my pocket. Instead, I reached in and flipped the switch that would prevent it from doing it again. There wasn't anything more important than being with Maisie. Whatever else was happening in the world, someone else could handle.

"Ranger?" A sweet, soft voice woke me. I opened my eyes and looked into Maisie's.

"Hi, beautiful."

"I need to use the restroom."

"Of course." I eased my body from hers and got off the gurney to help her up. She was wobbly on her feet, probably from the effects of the drugs Edwards had injected into her system.

As I waited for her to come out, I thought about the people I'd been forced to kill during my time with the CIA and after. Most were nameless and faceless. They stood between me and the person I was there to extract. If I hadn't killed them first, they would've taken my life along with as many of my teammates as they could.

I'd asked for Edwards to be kept alive because we needed information from him. Otherwise, I would've been happy to see a bullet between his eyes. Except in this case, it wasn't kill or be killed.

Maisie came out of the bathroom, and I helped her back to the gurney. She'd just lain down when someone arrived with a wheelchair to take her to a room. I took a step back so the man could help her into the chair and get the IV pole positioned.

"Ranger?"

"Right here."

"Are you coming with me?"

I stepped around so I was next to her. "Always."

When we got on the elevator, I held her hand, and when we got to the room, I didn't take a step back. I was the one to help her into bed. Once she was settled,

I crawled in next to her and wrapped my arm around her waist. She turned so her back was to me, but I didn't mind.

"I was afraid," she whispered.

I wanted her to say more, but I didn't push. "I was too."

"I knew you'd find me."

I gave her a gentle squeeze, unable to admit how terrified I was I wouldn't be able to.

"What happened to him?"

"I can tell you he was apprehended. Beyond that, you have been my priority."

"He's alive?"

I wanted to see her face when I answered, but I wouldn't push that either. "He is. We are unsure if he had anything to do with three more reported kidnappings in the area."

"Will these charges against him be dropped like the others were?"

"I promise you, Edwards will never walk free again." Her question reminded me that I didn't have the answer as to why the securities fraud indictment had never happened. Nor did we know whether the man found dead in his apartment had committed suicide or if Maxim would possibly be facing a murder charge as well.

"Do you swear?"

"On my own life."

A few minutes later, she was asleep. With as little movement as possible, I pulled my cell phone out of my pocket. When I saw missed calls from both Diesel and Doc, I eased out from behind Maisie and went out into the hallway. I called Diesel first.

"Hey, how's Maisie?"

"I'm not sure how to answer that. Better than a few hours ago. Is that why you called?"

"No. Do you want an update on Edwards?"

I flexed both my hands and paced the hallway before finally responding. "I don't think so."

"Roger that."

"I told Doc I don't want to know where he is."

"Yeah, I got that memo."

"I swore to Maisie on my life that he'd never walk free again."

"The charges against him will help ensure that—if he lives long enough to face them."

"Diesel, I've been giving a lot of thought to how I feel on that subject."

"I get it."

"You do?" He didn't respond, but he didn't need to. Diesel knew me better than anyone. If he said he got it, he did.

Maisie was still asleep when I went back into her room, so I sent a text to Doc, asking about Al and Mary. He responded that he and Merrigan had taken them back to their camp, and while they were very worried about Maisie, they were thankful we'd found her and she was alive.

I sat in the room's recliner and must have drifted off, but woke when I heard Maisie whimpering. I moved to the edge of the bed. "Wake up, beautiful. You're having a nightmare," I soothed, rubbing her arm.

She jolted and looked into my eyes.

"It was a nightmare. You're safe."

Maisie nodded, and when I stretched out beside her, she rested in my arms with her head on my chest. This would be our new normal. For who knew how long.

I called Doc again, per Maisie's request, and asked if he and Merrigan would bring Al and Mary back. I also asked that they bring her a change of clothes and some toiletries since she'd be spending the night.

They arrived about an hour before I was due to meet with the therapist. If they hadn't, I would've rescheduled. For now, I wouldn't feel comfortable leaving Maisie alone.

"I'm going to talk with the psychologist at two," I told her.

"I saw her earlier. She said she hoped to meet with you to review a few things."

"There's something I need to tell you. The K19 team knows we're married. As does the hospital. I'm sorry, Maisie. I know you wanted to tell your grandparents first."

"I know. Someone came in and asked about my husband when we were in the emergency room, so I told them."

I sighed, not knowing what to say. I wished it hadn't been this way but for far more than her grandparents learning we'd eloped.

"I didn't tell them where, though. Maybe we could do that together."

My sigh of sadness turned into one of relief. I pulled out my phone and showed her the photo I'd made my screensaver. It was one Mabel had taken of us right after the ceremony. Maisie's eyes filled with tears, but she grabbed my hand when I lowered the phone.

"Let me see it again." She ran her finger over the image of us. "Can you have a print made?"

I told her I could.

"I want to be able to look at it."

On my way to see Ms. Fasano, I sent the photo to Diesel and asked that he not just have someone print it, but have them pick up a frame and bring it to the hospital.

The psychologist and I didn't discuss much that Doc and I hadn't earlier. She went over the things outlined in the survivor support literature in the same way he had, reiterating that Maisie needed to process what had happened to her in her own time and in her own way.

"My understanding is you haven't been married very long."

I shrugged one shoulder. "It doesn't matter when it starts when you know you'll love someone for the rest of your days."

"That's a very romantic notion."

"If your definition of 'notion' is that we were impulsive, I'd like to suggest you consider that you know very little about Maisie and me. In fact, you know nothing about us at all."

"I beg to differ."

"You know about something that happened to Maisie. A vile, horrific thing that will never define who she is."

"You are naive when it comes to the impact of rape."

"Miss, if you knew a thing about me, naive would be the last word you would use." I leaned forward and put my elbows on my knees. "Earlier, I thought about how she and I would look at this time of our lives. How we'd define it. We have choices. One is that we look at it as the time before and after her abduction. Another is as the time before we fell in love and after we committed our lives to each other." My eyes bored into hers. "Maisie means everything to me, and I will make it my mission to spend every day celebrating the commitment we made and the love we share."

The condescending grin and the way she tilted her head, as though she felt sorry for my naivete, made me feel sorry for her. "Maybe one day you'll be lucky enough to know what I'm talking about."

25

Ranger

"You okay?" Diesel asked when I got off the elevator.

I shook my head. "Yeah."

He rubbed my shoulder.

"What are you doing here?"

He handed me a bag with tissue paper sticking out of the top of it. "I'm assuming this is for Maisie."

I moved the paper aside so I could see the framed photograph. "Thanks, man. I hope you didn't think I was asking you to do this and certainly not in an hour."

"Figured if you wanted her to have it, sooner would be better. By the way, it's a great photo. You can feel the love just by looking at it."

"Right? Maybe if the woman I just got done talking to had seen it, she would've had a clue about how things really are between Maisie and me."

"Seen what?" Ms. Fasano asked, stepping out of the other elevator.

"Nothing," I muttered. "Was there something else you needed?"

"I have patients, Mr. Messick. Your wife is one of them."

"Her family is with her now. You might want to come back later."

She walked past Diesel and me and straight into Maisie's room.

"Bitch," I said under my breath.

"She might be, but damn, she's a pretty one."

"Hadn't noticed."

"Listen, there are some things I need to bring you up to speed on. Since Al and Mary are with Maisie, and now the doc is too, I thought you might be able to get away for a few minutes."

While I didn't want to be away from my wife any longer than necessary, Diesel wouldn't ask if it weren't important.

"I'll just check in, and then, yeah, we can talk." I handed him back the bag with the photo. When I gave it to her, I wanted to be able to sit and talk about what that night meant to me and, I hoped, to her.

When I stuck my head in the door, Mary was sitting beside Maisie on the bed, stroking her hair. My heart nearly burst with joy when I noticed her smile at something Al said. The psychologist was smiling too.

"Sorry to interrupt. I have something to take care of real quick, but I'll be back in a few minutes."

Maisie held her hand out to me, and I walked over to the bed, leaned down, and kissed her.

"I'll wait until you get back to tell them," she whispered.

"I'll hurry."

Diesel was standing by the elevator when I returned. "Better to go downstairs."

Instead of stopping on the lobby level, Diesel pressed the button for the lower parking garage. When we stepped out, I saw a black SUV parked a few feet away and got in the passenger side.

"What have you got?" I asked when he was seated on the driver's side.

"First, Manhattan's soon-to-be-former district attorney was arrested this afternoon on charges of bribery, public corruption, obstruction of justice, and violation of oath of office in connection with Edwards' securities fraud indictment."

"No shit? He buried it?"

"Tried to, anyway. He and Edwards go way back. Childhood friends, I guess." He shrugged. "Next up is we got an ID on the guy you took out in the tunnel.

Name's Tony Paularino. He had *strong* ties to the Bonanno family, if you know what I mean."

The Bonannos were one of what was known as the Five Families—the major organized crime families of the Italian-American Mafia. They operated mainly in Brooklyn, Queens, Staten Island, and Long Island, but also had influence in Manhattan, the Bronx, and Westchester County.

"Why was Edwards working with a guy connected to one of the five families? Not to mention bribing the Manhattan district attorney?"

"The fucker is psychotic."

"Don't even suggest it. I don't want him getting off on an insanity plea."

"Before I forget, there was also an ongoing FBI investigation into March's connection to the Bonannos."

"Who is March?"

"The Manhattan DA."

"Did Agent Davies tell you all this?"

"It was like she won the damn lottery when she made the connection between March and Edwards. The feds have been trying to prove the Bonannos had March in their pocket for months."

"What about the other victims?"

Diesel shook his head. "I don't think it was Edwards, Range. Neither does Agent Davies. More likely it was a copycat."

"Even with the Hanover connection?"

"Could be a coincidence. A high percentage of high school graduates in the Adirondack area end up there or in Burlington at the University of Vermont."

I studied him. "You're sure?"

Diesel shook his head. "I'm not. What I said is I don't *think* it was him."

"How did Edwards get mixed up with the likes of Paularino? Was it March's connection to the Bonannos?"

"This is where it gets interesting. You told me Maisie was in a relationship with Edwards when they were in college but she ended it when she found out he was seeing someone else. Well, apparently, it wasn't just anyone else. It was Tony Paularino's cousin."

"Lemme guess. She's also connected to the Bonannos?"

"Tony's mother's sister married Tito Bonanno."

"*Jesus.* Tito's an underboss."

"Now you know what I meant by strong ties."

"Who's with Edwards now?"

"We brought in a couple of guys."

I hung my head and shook it. I didn't want to know the details of the *interrogation*. What I wanted was to tie him to the other murders and put an end to the Adirondack serial killing.

"What makes you think he isn't responsible for the other victims?"

"Working theory is that he heard about the other kidnappings, probably from March, and that's where he got the idea."

"The idea? You mean to kidnap Maisie? Why?"

He looked out the driver's side window, then back at me. "We have reason to believe he intended to use the ransom money to disappear."

"And take her with him?"

"There's evidence to strongly suggest it."

Fuck. I couldn't even let myself think about that scenario.

"What's Onyx's take?"

Diesel looked out the driver's side window for the second time.

"What?"

"He's one of the guys we brought in."

Onyx Yáñez had a lot of talents that had made him very valuable to the CIA back in the day and more valuable to K19 now.

When I told Maisie I'd follow him into any battle, anywhere, anytime, I meant every word. Until the plane crash that had almost ended his life, he was a pilot—once one of the most revered fighter pilots in the military. He was also an explosives expert and, most importantly to this investigation, a master interrogator. If anyone could get Edwards to talk, he could.

"I gotta get back up there."

Diesel nodded.

I grabbed the bag with the photo, opened the door, but didn't get out. "What's the evidence?"

"What do you mean?"

"That he intended to take her with him?"

"Ranger—"

"Tell me."

"Fake passports, other identification."

"For?"

"A husband and wife."

26

Maisie

Ranger did a good job of hiding it, but I knew something was wrong the minute he returned to the room. More wrong than when he'd left.

He walked straight over to the bed and leaned down to kiss me, just like he had earlier.

"Hi," I said when he pulled back and looked into my eyes.

"I love you."

I brought my hand to his cheek. "I love you too."

"I have something for you."

"What?"

He pulled a bag from behind his back and handed it to me. When my grandmother got up from the other side of the bed and sat in a chair, Ranger sat on the opposite side of me.

I reached in and pulled out a frame. In it was the photo he'd shown me on his phone.

"Where? How?"

"Diesel."

"Is he still here? Can I thank him?"

Ranger shook his head. "He had to get back."

The tension I'd seen when he walked in, the one he'd covered up when he kissed me, was evident again.

"Should we tell them now?" he asked.

It took me a second to figure out what he meant. "Oh. Right." I turned the photo around so it faced my grandparents. "This was taken the night we were married."

Grandma Mary gasped and reached for the frame. "You look so beautiful, Maisie." She handed it to my grandfather. "Doesn't she, Al?"

There were tears in his eyes. "She looks so much like you when we eloped. Even the dress is similar."

She gasped a second time. "It is."

"Ranger and I got married at the Love Lodge on Long Lake."

Both of their heads shot up. "You did?" asked Grandpa Al.

"We did," answered Ranger.

"Do you remember someone named Mabel from when you were married there?"

My grandmother looked confused.

"You did get married there, right?"

"We did."

"Mabel's parents owned the lodge back then. She said she remembers you."

"I don't recall."

"It's okay, Grandma. The important thing is that Ranger and I got married there too, but until Mabel told me, I hadn't realized it was where you'd eloped."

"You remember," said my grandfather. "When we went back for our twentieth anniversary, she and her husband were running the place. They hadn't been married that long. I can't remember his name, though."

"Charlie MacIntosh."

"Dipper?" Ranger asked.

"That's right. Mabel said his real name is Charlie."

"Well, my goodness. This is quite the story, Maisie Ann. What a wonderful coincidence! And you say you didn't realize that's where we wed?"

"I didn't, Grandma, but when we got there, it looked so familiar."

She looked at the photo once more before handing it back to me. I saw her eyes were full with tears.

"We should all go there together," I said, looking at Ranger.

"Definitely." He ran his finger over the photo. "Most definitely."

I rested my head on Ranger's shoulder and closed my eyes.

"Al, we should head back to the camp now."

While I was in no hurry for them to leave, I didn't argue when they stood to go.

"We'll see you tomorrow, sweetheart," she said, patting my hand.

"Good night, Maisie Ann," said my grandfather as they walked toward the door. "We love you so much. You too, Ranger."

"That was sweet," he said once they were gone.

"Thank you for my photo."

"You're welcome."

I set it on the table beside the bed and turned my body so I could rest my head against my husband's chest. "What happened when you were gone?" I felt him tense, but only for a second.

"Nothing important."

I looked up at him. "I understand you may be trying to protect me, but don't do it by lying to me."

He stroked my hair. "Diesel told me some things about Edwards. It isn't anything you need to know right now."

"Something in particular upset you."

He took a deep breath and let it out slowly. "Maisie—"

"Please just tell me. It'll be worse if you don't."

"I think he intended to try to take you out of the country."

I raised my hand to my temple and pressed with my fingertip. It was as though there was a memory I could almost reach out and grasp, but then it would slip away.

"What is it?" Ranger asked.

"Something he said."

"It's okay, don't…think about it."

"No, I need to. What was it?" I closed my eyes. They were the last words he spoke to me. "He said, 'It'll be enough money for us to disappear forever.'"

Ranger tightened his arms around me. "I can't believe how close I came to losing you."

"But you didn't. You found me."

He wiped away a tear. "I'm supposed to be comforting you, not the other way around."

I shook my head. "We're supposed to comfort each other."

When the nurse came in the next morning, she woke both Ranger and me and told him he couldn't sleep in the hospital bed with me. Evidently, the night nurse hadn't thought it was a big deal.

He got up to use the restroom, and when he came out, she was gone.

"She said the doctor is making rounds and should be here soon."

He climbed in next to me. "Then, I have a few more minutes."

I know I woke both of us several times throughout the night with my nightmares, but afterwards, I couldn't remember much about them. The psychologist said they would diminish quickly since most of what I dreamed was what my subconscious "invented" rather than an actual memory, since I'd been kept drugged the majority of the time Maxim held me captive. It made sense, given when I was awake, I remembered very little.

It took Ranger's prompt of saying he believed Maxim had intended to take me out of the country for me to remember what he'd said about "us" disappearing together. I wondered how many other memories would be jarred loose with prompts. I hoped none at all.

When the door opened, Ranger got off the bed and sat in the chair next to it.

He looked groggy but sexy, like he had when we'd wake up and make love in the middle of the night while on our trip. The sexy part surprised me, but then, rape wasn't sex. It was a violent assault that, thankfully, I couldn't recall much of.

"How are you feeling this morning?" the doctor I'd first seen in the emergency room asked.

"Tired, and I still have a headache."

He checked my heart rate and breathing with a stethoscope even though there were machines attached to me, doing the same thing.

"The toxicology report came back this morning. You were given Mistanprodol. It's a relatively new drug. To humans anyway. It's similar to Rohypnol, also known as the date-rape drug, but much more powerful in that it will render a victim unconscious rather than just take away decision-making skills and short-term memory."

"What kind of side effects do we need to be watching for?" Ranger asked.

"Headaches primarily and nightmares. It leaves the system relatively quickly, which often makes it difficult to detect since it doesn't show up in most tox screens." He looked at me. "In your case, you were injected with it not too long before you were brought in, so there was still enough in your system for us to identify it."

"When do you think my wife can be released?"

"As long as the headache doesn't get worse, later this morning. Upon discharge, you'll be given a watch list. If anything on it occurs, you'll have to come back to the hospital." He looked from me to Ranger. "Any other questions?"

There was nothing else I could think of and said so. Ranger said he couldn't think of anything, either.

When the doctor left, my husband lay down next to me and put his arm around my waist. "We need to talk about where you want to go after they say you can leave."

We did? Wouldn't we just go back to his camp? "What are my options?"

"Wherever you want, including leaving the Adirondacks."

"Is that what you think I should do?"

"It's entirely up to you. My main objective is for you to feel safe."

"I don't think leaving my home is a good idea."

"Then, we won't."

"I know you said Maxim is in custody, but didn't you also tell me Blanca and Jimmy said there were two men?"

"The other is no longer a threat."

"What does that mean?"

"He's dead." I shuddered, and he studied me. "I want to answer your questions honestly, but I don't want to go too far. That may have been."

"No. It wasn't. I'm glad he's dead. I only wish Maxim was too." Ranger didn't respond. "What will happen to him?"

"Right now, he's still being interrogated. Once we determine what he'll be charged with, he'll go into custody, probably with the FBI." He put his thumb and finger on my chin. "The other thing I learned yesterday is that the man responsible for the securities fraud charges disappearing was also apprehended. Given the number of counts against him and his flight risk, he will likely not be granted bail when he appears before a judge."

"Will that be true for Maxim too?"

"Even more true."

"I have more questions."

I felt Ranger's head nod, and he stroked my hair. "I'll answer as many as I can."

"I don't want you to keep things from me. I want to know what's going on."

"I understand. You need to take this at your own pace, and I'll do my best to be right there with you. That includes giving you answers."

Whatever questions I thought I had, I couldn't remember. What I did recall was someone—maybe the doctor who just left—telling me I would have short-term memory issues, but they would get better as the drugs Maxim gave me left my system.

"I think I'll close my eyes for a bit."

Ranger kissed my forehead. "Me too."

27

Ranger

I was anxious to find out what else Onyx was able to get out of Edwards overnight. Sleep deprivation was a common technique used during interrogations— among other less *innocuous* things.

Despite everything Diesel said about Maxim's abduction of Maisie being a copycat kidnapping, I still held out hope the man was responsible for the other serial killings. If the outcome was different, Maisie might *not* feel safe going home.

Canada Lake meant so much to her that she'd worked tirelessly to revitalize its economy. I wanted to witness her careful planning coming to fruition, including the redevelopment of the amusement park, the hotel, and the boardwalk. They were all things that would bring her great pride and joy throughout her life.

Selfishly, I wanted to raise a family and for our children to be able to experience the lake in the way Maisie's grandparents and mine had.

It occurred to me that Doc hadn't said anything about Maisie's ability to get pregnant. As thorough as he usually was, I expected he would have if he or the doctors believed it would be an issue. I prayed not. Maisie would be an amazing mother to any child we were blessed with.

One other thing I was uncertain about was whether Maisie would still feel safe once we got back to my camp. Would it trigger memories?

Before we got there, I wanted our team to beef up the security system. Both there and to install a complete setup at Al and Mary's.

I pulled out my cell and sent a text to Diesel, asking him to talk it over with Onyx and see how quickly we could make that happen.

Until we were able to catch the serial killer—and we would—I wanted to keep as many of our team in Canada Lake as Onyx would allow. That number would vary depending on what other assignments we were given. At times, all available team members would be required to engage, like they had when looking for Maisie. What would I do if I was required to leave?

If I had to answer today, I would refuse. Refusing would also mean I might have to resign my position with K19 Shadow Ops. If it came to that, I would. Maisie was my priority above all else. I couldn't envision a time I would be comfortable leaving her alone even for a few hours, let alone days. As Diesel said, we were protectors. It was in our blood, our DNA, and nothing would change something so innate.

Jesus—DNA. Maisie had told me she was on birth control, which wasn't one hundred percent effective, regardless of the type. Couple that with the possibility the drugs Edwards gave her had a negative interaction with the contraceptives, and the worst possible outcome was that we would find out she was pregnant. I said a silent prayer to God not to let that happen.

When the door opened a little after eight, I expected to see a nurse rather than Ms. Fasano. When she spoke, Maisie woke.

"I understand you'll be going home this morning," she said, handing Maisie a card and shooting me a look. "I'd like to schedule a follow-up appointment in the next couple of days."

I was sure there were other psychologists who specialized in post-assault therapy. Maybe one closer in distance to the camp.

"By the way, I have a place on the channel, so if you'd prefer to meet at my home office, we can do that too."

The channel? Shit. That had to mean the one right off Canada Lake, which was minutes from my place. *Our* place, I silently corrected myself.

"That would be better," I heard Maisie say. "Would it be possible to schedule something tomorrow?"

Fasano pulled out her phone. "I'm free in the morning. How does ten sound?"

When I failed to keep myself from sighing, both women looked at me.

"What?" Maisie asked.

"I'm just afraid you won't be up for it."

"If she's not, I'll come to her."

While I had an increasing dislike of the woman, Maisie didn't seem to. I needed to set my feelings aside and do what was best for my wife.

"Can you stick around for a minute?" I asked her.

"Of course."

I gave Maisie a kiss and went into the hallway to call Diesel. When I did, I saw I'd missed a call from Onyx from a few minutes ago.

"Morning," I said when he picked up.

"Ranger. Thanks for getting back to me so quickly."

"Of course. Sorry I didn't see your call earlier. What's going on?"

"We're getting ready to turn Edwards over to FBI custody. Before we do that, I want to be sure we didn't miss any questions you wanted answered."

"I'm sure you covered it, boss. What's your take on whether or not he abducted and killed the other women?"

"I don't think it was him, as much as we all wish it were. The only definitive answer will be if the murders stop happening. Even then it isn't a sure thing. Whoever the killer is may stop for a while, knowing the investigation is getting more intense, or stop altogether."

I knew there were instances when serial killers didn't strike for several years before picking up again.

The longer we went without knowing if it was Edwards or someone else, the longer it was left an unknown. Unknowns caused fear. It would be especially true for Maisie, but equally so for me.

My first instinct was to take her away from the park, out of the state, or even the country. But that wasn't up to me. Maisie needed to be in control of her own life. The last thing I could make her feel was powerless.

After my call with Onyx ended, I placed another one to Diesel.

"Heard the boss talking to you just now," he said.

"Yeah. I hear you're getting ready to turn him over to the bureau."

"I volunteered to be part of the transport team."

Something about that worried me. "Godspeed, my friend."

"Thanks, Range. What's happening there?"

"Fasano is in with Maisie now. The doctor was in earlier and said he thought she could go home this morning."

"You'll need transport."

"That's right."

"I'll ask Onyx to reassign the transport team. Do you want me to head there now?"

"Nah. The discharge process may take a while." I wanted to argue and say it wasn't necessary for him to be the one to pick us up, but my gut was telling me Diesel shouldn't be part of Edward's extradition.

"Copy that."

I was about to end the call when Diesel spoke again. "On the subject you messaged me about earlier, increasing security at your place and setting it up at the Jones' camp was already in process. My understanding is Doc facilitated making it happen."

Since Doc's father was a security and technology genius, whom governments hired if he agreed to take on the jobs, I had no doubt whatever security was in place at Al and Mary's and at my camp, would be as good as what was at the White House.

After our call ended, I leaned up against the wall outside Maisie's room long enough to get my composure in check. It had been obvious in the last few hours that my wife could read me more than I believed anyone could.

When I felt ready, I opened the door. Good thing since it appeared Fasano was anxious to leave.

"We'll talk tomorrow," she said on her way out.

"Hey, beautiful." I walked over, sat on the edge of the bed, and took Maisie's hand in mine. "Things are set for when we leave. Diesel will come get us. My guess is Swan will be with him."

"I like her."

I was glad to hear it. Not everyone did. The woman could be abrasively British at times.

"You'll probably be seeing a lot of her."

"Ranger?"

"Yeah?"

"You're taking me home, right? I mean to your place."

"Our place, but yes. If that's where you want to go. I'll understand if you'd rather be at your grandparents' camp."

Her eyes opened wide. "Is that what you want?"

"Not at all. We already talked about this. My only desire is that you're comfortable, but yes, I want us to be *home.* Together. Forever."

"That's what I want too." She bit her lip, and her eyes filled with tears.

"Tell me what you're feeling."

"Ms. Fasano warned me that I may not be experiencing the worst of my response to what happened to me yet."

I took a deep breath, hoping Maisie didn't pick up on my anger.

"You don't like her."

I smiled. So much for hiding anything from her. "I do not."

"What if she's right?"

"Here's what I think. There no way to predict whether things will be easier or harder on you. I would assume it'll be both. Whatever you need, want to talk about, don't want to talk about, want to do, or not do, I'm your guy." I remembered Doc's words to me. "I'm your safe place, Maisie. You'll never have to worry about what I think or how I'll react."

She nodded.

"You're *safe* with me, beautiful," I repeated.

"That's the way I feel."

Nothing she said could have relieved me more. Especially when she was so good at picking up on my feelings. If she felt safe with me, that meant she truly believed she was. Right now, it was all that mattered.

28

Ranger

We were in the SUV on our way back to the camp when both my phone and Diesel's went off with an emergency alert we knew meant our immediate attention was required. As soon as he could, he pulled to the side of the road.

"Ranger checking in," I said when Onyx answered my call.

"Ranger, all hell has broken loose on Edward's transport. The team was ambushed. Edwards was taken out. Two agents are down, but I haven't been able to determine who or what their condition is."

My stomach lurched when I thought about my premonition about Diesel being on that transport. The man was like a brother to me. Most of the K19 team was, but I was closest to him.

"Copy that. Diesel, Maisie, and I are almost back to the camp. What do you need from me?"

"High alert. *Do not* return to your camp until you get the all clear from me."

I was sitting in the backseat with Maisie but had the phone on speaker so Diesel could hear the call. I put one arm around her and brought her closer to me when I felt her tremble.

"Any other parameters?"

"Negative. Let me know where you land."

"Where did the ambush take place?"

"Albany field office."

"Copy that."

"West?" asked Diesel when I hung up.

It was either that or north, but until we got the all clear that this was an isolated incident intended solely to take out Edwards, I wouldn't retrace any of our recent travels.

"My folks have a place on Oneida Lake," Diesel reminded me.

"That works." It was two hours from where we were now, and there was a possibility we'd have the okay to go home before we even got there. However, it gave us a place to stay if we needed it.

"How are you doing, beautiful?" I brought Maisie as close to me as I could get her with the constraints of our seat belts.

"Maxim is dead?"

"He is."

"Who would've done this?"

My eyes met Diesel's in the rearview, and he gave me a head nod.

"What we've learned in the last couple of days is that Edwards was mixed up with some dangerous criminals. My guess is they believed he might offer to talk in exchange for having some of his charges reduced."

Her eyes opened wide. "Charges reduced? Oh my God."

I squeezed her shoulders. "First, just because the people who killed him may have feared it might happen, it doesn't mean it would've. Second, he's dead, so it's no longer an issue."

"Right. Thank God."

I wasn't sure what exactly she was thankful for, but I had my own appreciation to offer up. Thank God Edwards was dead. Thank God Diesel didn't get caught in the crossfire. And finally, I would never stop being thankful Maisie was safe.

"While I know you wanted to go home as much as I did, you're in for a real treat. Diesel's parents' lake house is really nice."

"It was built in the twenties," he said. "More of a house than a camp. It has seven bedrooms and is fully winterized."

"Wait until you see it. It doesn't have a dock; it has a pier."

Maisie's eyes opened wide like they had before, but this time she was smiling. "I can't wait to see it."

I hoped Diesel wouldn't mind if we still went there, even if we did get clearance to return to Canada Lake. It would be a nice divergence.

Fortunately, when I'd asked Doc to ask Maisie's grandparents to bring her a change of clothes and toiletries, they brought more than one, and Merrigan even thought to pick up a few things for me from my camp. If necessary, Diesel could wear some of my clothes. It certainly wouldn't be the first time we borrowed from each other.

"I doubt there's food at my parents' place, but there's a restaurant nearby called the Boathouse. I don't know about you two, but I'm starving, and they have great food."

Diesel pulled in when we said we were hungry too. I immediately knew it would go on Maisie's list of places to emulate, and I was grateful to my friend for giving her the distraction.

While we were sitting at the bar, waiting for a table, Maisie got up to look at some of the historic photos hanging on the wall.

"There's something I need to tell you," I said to Diesel.

"Yeah?"

"My gut told me you shouldn't be on the transport team."

He raised a brow. "No shit?"

I shook my head.

"Fuck. Well, thanks." He raised his beer to mine, and we toasted.

"Not the first time it's happened between us."

"No, Ranger, it sure isn't."

"Have you heard anything from Onyx?"

"Rodriguez."

"Condition?"

Diesel shook his head.

"Damn. I didn't know him very well, but whenever we lose one of the good guys, it always sucks." I brought my beer bottle back to his. "To Rodriguez."

"Agent Davies was also hit."

My eyes opened wide. "Condition?"

"Still in surgery."

The way he said it, sounded more *personal* than I'd expected. "Sorry to hear that, man."

He looked out the window into the darkness. "Thanks, Range."

"Listen, I know I've been pretty self-involved lately. I want you to know I'm sorry."

Diesel laughed. "It's all good, buddy."

Maisie returned to the bar but didn't take a seat. Instead, she stood behind me and draped her arms over my shoulders. I turned my head, and we kissed.

"Your table is ready," said the bartender who came out from behind the bar with menus in her arms.

"Looks like it's kind of slow tonight. If it would be easier on you if we sat at the bar, we're happy to," offered Maisie.

"I was just going to seat you over here." She pointed to a table a few steps away from where we were.

Diesel nodded.

"We'll stay put," I told her. I knew exactly what Maisie was up to. If we sat at the bar, she could pick the bartender's brain. And that meant her mind wouldn't be on Maxim or any of the other shit she'd gone through.

We ended up staying at the Boathouse until closing time, but the place we were staying in was within walking distance—if it wasn't the middle of winter. So, in this case, it meant a quick drive. When we walked inside, there was a fire going and several of the lights were turned on.

"Caretaker lives over the garage," Diesel explained.

I opened the fridge to put away our leftovers from dinner and saw it was well-stocked. "Looks like we've got the makings for breakfast."

I looked over when Diesel didn't answer and saw he was reading something on his phone.

"Everything okay?"

"Yeah. Bryar is out of surgery, and her condition has been upgraded to stable."

Bryar? Oh! Agent Davies. "That's great news, man."

"Onyx says we're clear to return to the lake whenever we're ready."

While I might've suggested we stay on a couple of days so Maisie could see more of the area, I sensed Diesel might want to get back as soon as possible.

"We can skip breakfast if you want to get on the road earlier tomorrow."

Diesel was still looking at his phone. "Nah, we can have breakfast."

"I'm supposed to meet with Patricia tomorrow. I completely forgot," said Maisie.

"I'm sure you could reschedule for later in the day or the following one. I can give her a call and leave a message."

"You wouldn't mind?"

"Calling? Of course not."

I hung up after leaving the psychologist a voicemail telling her we needed to change the meeting time and saw Maisie yawn.

"You're probably exhausted. Let's find our room and call it a night."

"Second door at the top of the stairs," said Diesel, getting a beer out of the fridge.

"See ya in the morning."

"Yep."

"Is he okay?" Maisie asked once we were in the room.

"The FBI agent who has been working with us was one of the people shot earlier today. Diesel was her point person, so it probably jarred him."

"It seems like more."

I pulled her into my arms. "Tell me why."

She shrugged. "He looked at his phone a lot during dinner. It seemed unusual."

"I picked up on a little something when he told me she was out of surgery." I wiggled my eyebrows, and Maisie smiled, but it faded quickly.

"Ranger, I'm not sure about…you know."

I led her over to the bed, sat on the end, and pulled her onto my lap. "We are going to take this slow, Mrs. Messick."

"But—"

I shook my head. "You are here with me. I get to hold you in my arms. Do you know how happy that makes me?"

Maisie wrapped her arms around my neck, and I could feel the dampness of her tears. "If it weren't for you, I might've…"

"Shh. You're here now. That's all that matters."

Maisie and I had spent several nights together, but even in the hospital bed, she hadn't clung to me like she did last night. I didn't mind. It seemed to help with the nightmares or, as either the doctor or Fasano—I couldn't remember which—had said, they were happening less and less frequently as time went on.

"I'd like to come back to this area sometime," Maisie said when we were getting in the SUV.

"I think that could be arranged." I winked.

"You can sit in front with Diesel if you want. I'll be okay."

"Heck no! I'm the boss, remember? I've waited a long time to have someone chauffeur me around."

Diesel laughed and shook his head. "You're so full of crap."

While I wished I could put it off, Maisie needed to know about the three other kidnappings that had taken place within the Adirondack Park and also that the women abducted were murdered. I'd planned to tell her once we returned to Canada Lake yesterday, but my gut was telling me I shouldn't wait any longer. Who knew how long it might be before the media got a hold of the story, as well as Maisie's. That is not how I wanted her to find out.

"There's something we need to talk about before we get home," I began.

Her eyes met mine.

In the most straightforward way I could, I told her about the three women kidnapped before she was. Her first question, as I'd anticipated, was whether Maxim was responsible.

"Can I answer?" asked Diesel.

I nodded.

He told her he'd been part of the interrogation team and neither he nor anyone else, including Agent Davies, believed Edwards was responsible.

"Unfortunately, we believe Maxim used the other kidnappings as a cover for what he did to you."

Surprising me, like she so often did, Maisie hugged me tight. "Thank God for you," she whispered, then leaned forward. "You too, Diesel."

He smiled.

29

Maisie

It had been four days since Ranger left a message for Patricia and we still hadn't heard back from her.

When he called the hospital, they said she hadn't been in her office much this week but it wasn't unusual and that she set her own hours.

Maybe I hadn't read her right the couple of times I met her, but her ghosting us seemed odd. Ranger and I talked about it and agreed to look for someone else. He even admitted he wanted someone to talk to too, and it made me love him more.

On the surface, we were all acting like everything was *fine*, but it wasn't. I hoped the day would come when I didn't have flashbacks of what Maxim did to me, but I wasn't naive enough to think it would happen quickly.

The first day we were back, I'd expected Ranger to coddle me. I was so relieved when he didn't. He would reassure me that he was there for whatever I needed, didn't push me to talk, and when I wanted to, he listened. While I knew he wasn't perfect, it was becoming increasingly harder to find anything wrong with him.

My cell phone rang at the same time Ranger's did, which was unusual. I'd gotten used to it when it happened between Diesel and him.

"Hey, Grandma," I said when I saw her name pop up.

"Hi, sweetheart."

Her voice sounded funny. "What's wrong? Is Grandpa okay?"

"Grandpa is fine. I just wondered if you happen to be watching the television."

That was an odd question. I almost never did. "No. Why?"

"It's nothing. I just wondered. I'll talk to you later, sweetie."

I looked at the phone, stunned that she'd ended our call so abruptly. "Ranger?"

He came out from around the corner, and I could see he was still talking to someone. A few seconds later, there was a knock at the back door. He answered it before I could, and Onyx walked in.

"Hey, sis," he said, coming over to hug me. A minute or two later, Diesel arrived with Wasp and Swan.

"Should I go upstairs?" I asked Onyx since Ranger was still on the phone.

"Nah, you can stay down here with us for now."

Finally, Ranger put his cell phone down and walked over to where I sat in the living room. Everyone else was still standing.

"Can you give us a minute?" he asked, and the four other people in the room walked out to the sun porch.

"You're frightening me," I admitted. "First my grandmother. Now you."

Ranger gathered me in his arms. "That is the last thing I want to do, and I'm sorry."

"What is going on?"

"There's been another abduction."

"Oh God, no!" I gasped, and he held me tighter. Tears ran down my cheeks, and I started to shake.

"Shh," he soothed. "I know how hard this is for you. Just take a few deep breaths, and we'll talk it through."

What started as crying turned into sobs. I hadn't cried so hard since the day in the emergency room when my grandparents were there.

After a few minutes, I took a deep breath and regained my composure. "I'm sorry. I didn't expect it would affect me so profoundly."

"Don't be sorry, and I'm not surprised." He kissed my forehead. "It hits very close."

I rested my head on his shoulder and took several more deep breaths.

"You said your grandmother called?"

"She asked if I was watching television. It was weird because she knows I almost never do."

Ranger motioned, and Onyx came in from the porch. "The media may have picked up on this."

"Dammit," he muttered. He pulled out his phone and typed something before returning to the porch.

"They can come inside."

"Actually, it'll probably be better if I join them."

"I can go upstairs if I'm not allowed to hear what you're talking about."

Ranger squeezed my shoulders. "In this case, it isn't that. I'm more concerned about what we need to discuss upsetting you."

"If I can't handle it, I'll go up to our room. Okay?"

"My brave, beautiful wife. You amaze me."

I shook my head. "You're the one who's amazing."

He kissed me again and motioned to his teammates.

"Everyone okay if Maisie sits in on this?" he asked when the four of them sat down.

Onyx looked around the room. "We're good." He turned to me. "As long as you're good."

"I'll go upstairs if I feel uncomfortable."

Onyx's eyes met Ranger's.

"It's okay," my husband told him. "You can speak freely."

"Here is what we know," Onyx began. "At eleven hundred hours, Steve and Beth Fasano received a call demanding a ransom be paid."

I put my hand over my mouth to stifle my gasp.

"I'm sorry, Maisie," whispered Ranger. "There was no easy way to tell you."

"They were unaware their daughter was missing since she resides here at Canada Lake and they winter in West Palm Beach." Onyx looked at his phone, then raised his head. "Last known contact with Ms. Fasano was at Johnstown Memorial Hospital four days ago."

"We were the last people to see her?" I asked.

Onyx shook his head. "She saw several patients that day. We believe she left the hospital at a little after five. She hasn't been seen or heard from since."

Diesel cleared his throat. "I've been in contact with Agent Davies, who said her boss will arrive at the forestry lodge this afternoon. Since Ms. Fasano was likely abducted somewhere between the hospital and her house on the channel, this is as good a place as any for us to set up a command center."

"Copy that," said Onyx before turning to me. "How are you doing, Maisie?"

I took a deep breath. "I'm not sure how to answer. I'm terrified for Patricia, but we know it can't be Maxim who took her since he's dead."

"That's right." Onyx stood and looked at each of the other people in the room. "Okay, Shadow Ops, let's find Patricia Fasano and bring her home safe, just like we did with Maisie. And after that, we'll annihilate the motherfucker who took her."

Keep reading for a sneak peek

at the next book in the

K19 Shadow Operations Series—

DIESEL!

1

Diesel

Number four. That's how the FBI agent sent in to replace Special Agent Bryar Davies referred to the latest woman abducted by whom we now believed to be a serial killer. She wasn't a fucking number. She was a person.

The guy made me so angry with his disparaging label. I stormed out of the investigation command center. At first I only intended to walk down to the lake, but when I put my hand in my pocket to ward off the windchill of the Adirondacks in the middle of January and felt my key fob, I got in my SUV instead.

I didn't know exactly where I was going when I threw gravel, pulling out of the forestry service lodge where our investigation was based, only that I had to get the fuck out of there.

How the asshole the FBI sent in was Bryar's boss was a complete mystery. Even at her relatively young age of twenty-eight, she was twice the agent he was.

I was stunned when my cell rang and I saw the name of the very woman who was on my mind.

"How are you today, Agent Davies?" I answered.

"I just got a call from Ryan, saying you left without alerting anyone."

I shook my head. While *Ryan* may think he was in command of this case, he was in for a rude awakening when my bosses had enough of his shit and set him straight.

"I don't answer to him, babe."

"Don't be fucking smug with me, Diesel. This is the same dickhead power play shit you pulled with me the day I arrived."

"Guess you're feeling better." Agent Davies had taken a hit when the team transporting a prisoner was ambushed on the way to the FBI field office in Albany. She'd been in surgery for four hours and thirty-seven minutes before they were able to control the internal bleeding and repair the damage from the bullet that had ripped through her abdomen.

How did I know the exact amount of time she was in the operating room? Because I counted the fucking seconds. That's how.

Yeah, the woman was way under my skin. So god-damn far, I dreamed about her.

"Diesel? Are you still there?"

"Yeah, I'm here."

"Why did you say you guess I'm feeling better?"

"I don't think I've ever heard you toss so many swear words into one sentence."

"You haven't been listening."

"Where are you?"

"Still at the hospital, but they're talking about let-ting me leave today."

"I'll be there in twenty."

"Wait. No. You don't have to do that."

"Is someone else there with you?"

"No, but…"

"But, what? There aren't cabs in the Adirondacks, babe."

"I hate it when you call me that. Besides, aren't you anxious to get back to the investigation? I'm sure you're very concerned about locating your girlfriend and bringing her back safe."

"My girlfriend?" What the fuck was that about?

"You're not denying it."

"First of all, we're talking about a *person* who was abducted, probably by a serial killer. Second, Patricia Fasano is not my girlfriend."

"Not your girlfriend, but you slept with her."

"Those meds are messing with your head, babe. Never had a cup o' Joe with her, let alone sex."

"You have an IQ of what, in the one-sixties? Yet you use words like 'babe' and 'cup o' Joe.' You speak ten languages. Use better vocabulary."

"Twelve, and I'll see you in fifteen."

I ended that call and placed another, this time to my best friend, Ranger.

"Hey, I just got a call from the FBI asshole," he said.

"Yeah? What did he want?"

"To know where you are."

"Too fucking bad."

"Yeah. I appreciated the opportunity to tell him he wasn't your boss so it was none of his business. I used a few different words, but that was the gist." He chuckled. "But seriously. Where are you?"

"On my way to the hospital. Agent Davies thinks she might be released today."

"Would you cut the Agent Davies shit? Everyone else may be blind to how you hang on her every word, but I'm not. Her name is…what's her name?"

"Bryar."

"Yeah. Weird name. Anyway, so you're picking her up?"

"Yes, but that isn't why I called. For some reason, Bryar thinks I slept with the psychologist."

"Did you?"

"Fuck no."

"Why does she think you did?"

"I don't know, but I'm going to find out."

"On that subject, Onyx said something seemed off about the call Fasano's parents said they received. He wants to do some digging."

"Roger that. I'll get on it this afternoon."

"Already workin' it. Go get brier patch."

I laughed. She wasn't going to like that any better than babe.

I'd just gotten off the elevator on the surgical floor when Ranger called again.

"What's up?"

"Are you still on your way to the hospital?"

"Just got here, why?"

"Need you to head down to the ER as soon as possible."

Fuck. "Why?"

"Ms. Fasano has been located—alive."

"Where?"

"You'll never guess."

About the Author

USA Today and Amazon Top 15 Bestselling Author Heather Slade writes shamelessly sexy, edge-of-your seat romantic suspense.

She gave herself the gift of writing a book for her own birthday one year. Forty-plus books later (and counting), she's having the time of her life.

The women Slade writes are self-confident, strong, with wills of their own, and hearts as big as the Colorado sky. The men are sublimely sexy, seductive alphas who rise to the challenge of capturing the sweet soul of a woman whose heart they'll hold in the palm of their hand forever. Add in a couple of neck-snapping twists and turns, a page-turning mystery, and a swoon-worthy HEA, and you'll be holding one of her books in your hands.

She loves to hear from my readers. You can contact her at heather@heatherslade.com

To keep up with her latest news and releases, please visit her website at www.heatherslade.com to sign up for her newsletter.

MORE FROM AUTHOR HEATHER SLADE

Made in the USA
Columbia, SC
25 April 2022

59456083R00161